Lovesong

Lovesong

GWEN DAVIS

Doubleday Direct, Inc.   Garden City, New York

For Sherry who gave me Nadya who gave me Bali.
And for Jack, who taught me what it really meant.

Lovesong

And if I were to tell a tale
Of magic nights and golden sands
And two who looked with softened eyes
Upon a silver'd sea
Would there be those who said
"She loves what she has lost
And dreams of what can never be."
But if I sang a song from in my Soul
What difference
What they said of me?

THE FLAGS were up, suddenly. Triangular red and yellow flags stuck into bamboo poles on the sand, whipped in the all-at-once violent winds, warning bathers and boaters to stay away from the water. Fishermen who'd set out to sea when it was calm early that morning were specks on the darkening horizon now. And there were those who had straddled the waves on their surfboards, hoping for turbulent waters. But not this turbulent.

As she ran toward the roaring ocean, Karen could hear the whistles, the sirens signaling disaster. Grief, such an unfamiliar emotion once, something she'd had no preparation for the first time, pulled at her now like a despised friend who sought you out in a crowd though it was obvious you didn't want to have anything more to do with her.

"What is it?" she cried fearfully to the others running

on the sand. "What's happening?" she called out in one of the phrases she knew in their native tongue.

"Lost," moaned a brown-skinned man, loping toward the circle of people gathering in the distance.

"What? Who?" She tried to make herself heard above the howling of the wind, the shriek of the sirens. She was hardly audible to herself over the clutch in her throat, the pounding of her heartbeat in her ears.

He sprinted away, ignoring her. Or maybe he just did not know who was lost, or what.

Tearing across the sands, she prayed beneath her breath that it would not be everything.

One

LIKE MOST COUPLES, Karen and Charley had been so busy handling the intricacies of marriage, the major problems, the little irritations, laboring over how to keep love alive, it never occurred to them that one of them could die. When she lost him so suddenly, in what was still their prime, Karen foundered. She had considered herself an independent woman, taking pleasure from her songwriting, successful at it, hearing echoes of herself on the radio, imagining that her life as a career woman living in Manhattan was full even without the married part of it. Only with Charley gone did she fully grasp how much she had leaned on him, how balanced she had been by a loving, supportive male. She felt abandoned, enraged, as if his leaving had been voluntary. When at last her emotions began to settle, she understood that the great love she had always longed for she had actually had. She just hadn't known it at the time. And the music was gone from her, along with him.

Irredeemable, their moments together glowed brighter, adding feelings of waste to her sense of loss. How could she have missed so much of what they had together, hoping for different, or more? Yearning for the exotic, she hadn't realized how exotic it was simply to be cared for.

Grief had more or less disappeared from her face. The tight smile that pulled across her lips when she tried to seem braver than she felt was somewhat eased. Karen was still a pretty woman, chestnut hair curling loosely around her heart-shaped face, lively brown eyes as young as when she had first seen Charley. He'd been straightforward and hearty, not really her type. But his dedication to her was irresistible. No man in her life had ever been really *there* for her. Charley wanted to be nowhere else.

And then he was gone.

Making love was a skill she could not practice alone. She could still cook, and try to work at her music—to her numbed despair, she was unable to come up with even a melancholy song. And what Charley had been proudest of in her she could not do by herself. Not so there was art in it. Anymore than she could laugh, really laugh, aloud and long, alone.

Even while he'd lain dying and in the twilight hours

she recapped for him the highlights of what had been, she realized too late at last, a true love adventure, they laughed. She would hold him, her head on his wasting chest, and when the painkillers had little effect, try comforting him with melody, lullabies she made up as she sang.

"You're the most beautiful, most gifted woman in the world," he said, his fingers curling her hair. "But then, I'm on drugs."

So he'd stayed funny to the end. Even in his final coma, he chortled. It was as if the sense of humor that distinguished his life illuminated his death, and he got what a joke it was, all of it, people taking everything so seriously.

Her energy was undiminished, although having turned forty-two, according to the magazines she subscribed to, she was middle-aged. She studied little spiritual books from chain store checkout stands to quiet her longings, the womanly feelings that no longer had any outlet. Unseemly, she thought. Inappropriate for a widow with an almost-grown son.

Seth, her boy, was torn by his own sense of loss, mourning disguised as rage. He was at the age when all boys were difficult, waiting to go toe-to-toe with their fathers, to show "I'm as big a man as you." Since there was no one for Seth to go up against, he shadowboxed, fighting with a barrel-chested ghost, in a fury at his father for dying, angry with Karen for being solicitous and caring, at a time when a young man should be separating from his mother, not getting more connected to her. He'd been joined at the hip to his father and seemed resentful of Karen's attempts at closeness since Charley's death. She'd been caught up writing her music a lot of the years Seth would have welcomed the attention, and now he seemed unwilling to forgive her, to allow her to get close.

"What do you want for breakfast?" she asked him. He was at the kitchen table, his face deep in the sports pages, hair like a dark gold cloud above his high, furrowed brow.

"I'm not hungry," he said.

"Of course you are. You're still a . . ."

"I'm not a growing boy." Seth's hazel eyes looked at her, challenging. "They x-rayed my knees last week, and the bones have knitted."

"What does that mean?"

"It means I won't get any taller." There was in that pronouncement a flag of defeat, the hero who would never rise from the pack to throw the touchdown pass.

"You're tall enough," she said. He was better than tall enough: He was what she had considered in her teenage years a model of masculine beauty. The good-natured coarseness of Charley's features had been refined in his son into perfect angles and hollows, lending a soft cast to the unmistakably male countenance. Her own full mouth with its slightly brooding lower lip had been restamped on Seth. Only the gold-flecked eyes came from nowhere, some long-ago maybe Mongolian who had raped his genes into the strain. Mysterious eyes, wide set, Asian in cast. His body was lean, strong, a distilled version of his father's, the same barrel chest slightly sized down, with her slimness of hips. The hair that crowned it all was Charley's, but thicker, a renegade color, gold, like the flecks in his eyes.

"I'm not tall enough to suit the coach," he said.

"The coach is an idiot." The words came out of her as a reflex, Charley's words, an echo from Seth's freshman year when his father had stood where she stood now, by the refrigerator, cursing the unfairness of those put in charge of young people's lives.

"You don't even know him," Seth said.

"I'm coming to the game." Part of her recovery had involved avoiding football, the sound of it on TV, the sight of it on the field. As fond as she had been of her husband, as much as she loved her son, she had loathed the game, felt it jarring her eardrums and spirit all through her marriage. It was more than the roar and thuds and intrusive voices of the sportscasters that rankled her. Football seemed a place men could hide, never having to say what was on their minds. A boys' club that pretended women were invited, but where women weren't really welcome. And certainly not necessary.

Part of her resentment, she understood, was because of the intensity of the bonding that had taken place between father and son. Although relieved that Charley was involved in Seth's activities while she was busy writing her music, when she finished she longed to be with her son. But Sunday afternoons he was otherwise engaged: He and Charley would lie side by side on what was usually the marital bed, hurling epithets at the players on television, leaving a Hansel and Gretel–like trail of pretzel salt across the covers. Then there was the coaching connection formed when Seth was almost old enough to play, and his father would take him to the park to work out, get him into the championship form he was sure his son was going to have. Loving them, except for the exclusion and the noise, Karen had pretended to like football, giving Super Bowl parties, cooking gross food, the chili and hot dogs that went along with the game.

But they were on to her, her boys. They knew she hated it. After a while she stopped dissembling and went to the movies on Sundays, or for long walks, or into the little soundproofed studio she had rented on the top floor of their building, where she could play the piano, sing her pop songs, renourish her soul.

Still, as Charley was dying, so unlingeringly, not quite heart-attack sudden but fast of a slow disease, she would often close herself in their bathroom and sob, covering the sound with football, grateful, all at once, for the harsh clamor of Sundays and Monday nights. And when he was gone from his side of the bed, his ravaged face missing from the pillow, the game seemed to her a recrimination. Maybe if she had loved not just him but what he had loved, he would still be alive.

So she avoided the smallest reminder, or the biggest: the football practice on the field at Riverdale, Seth's getting himself up for the game. The first was to be this afternoon. Enough time had passed that there could be no excuse for her not going, especially with her son quarterbacking. "What time should I be there?"

"You don't have to come. Derek Miller is starting."

"But he's clumsy," she said, parroting Charley's appraisal. "He's a clown."

"He's six foot three," Seth said, swallowing, immortality no longer a possibility, out of his grasp by a couple of inches.

She gave him orange juice to help the anguish go down. "But you have all the moves for a great quarterback, the grace, the brains . . ."

"Stop trying to sound like Dad," he said, and drank the juice without tasting, like medicine.

She went to the game, making the bus trip to Riverdale as though it were easy for her, even pleasant. But the game itself depressed her. She saw it less as an athletic event than a ritual humiliation of her son, who sat round-shouldered on the bench, while the starting quarterback, the taller boy, threw terrible passes. All around her were fathers, still alive, next to wives who went shopping to satisfy their longings. Even while Karen tried not to think angry thoughts, they battered her. Bitterness had never been a part of her makeup, but then, she realized now, she had never had anything really to be bitter about. Life, even when her expectations let her down, had been filled with future possibilities. Now, everything seemed to be behind her.

The first chill winds of fall whipped leaves into the air. She wondered who would warm her. She tried to recall Charley's big, tender arm around her shoulders, struggled to remember his smell. He had prided himself on cleanliness, showering twice a day. His scent had been tinged with soap, baby-fresh-out-of-the-bath, but manly, musky, reassuring, as his arm had been, like his towering shadow. She had kept the last sweater he wore before the illness turned him sour, saved it in a drawer, refusing to send it to the Salvation Army with the rest of his things. Every once in a while when the ache became unbearable, she would put her face in it, as she had when it was still on his chest, and inhale what was left of his essence. But the sweater was starting to grow musty, take on ordinary odors, the wood of the drawer where it lay in tissue-papered isolation. Even the ghost of a man eventually gives up the ghost.

Hamlet's father would have come back to rail against the injustice. Seth's father would have been there, too, if he could have, striding the bleachers like battlements, booming his way to the football field, coming down to call the coach an asshole, cornering him at the half, using what had been his impressive bulk to lord over him the conviction he knew better, that it was *his* kid who ought to be in the game. And she suddenly wondered if that could be the reason the coach wasn't playing Seth—because Charley had opposed him, Charley had confronted him, and now Charley was no more. The tyranny of little men, whose only chance of winning was outliving their adversaries.

On the way home from the game, she was anxious, as she was always slightly fearful in New York, now that she was a woman alone, for all her love of the city. She had considered moving to the suburbs, Connecticut. But she did not want to put the strain of yet another jolt on Seth, to wrench her son anymore than life already had done.

He was so vulnerable. Even with his imposing size, if she squinted her eyes a certain way she could see once again the stocky little baby, full lower lip curved down at the corners. On the bus coming home, she resisted the impulse to hug him, for fear he would consider it consolation, rather than her own overwhelming affection, her need to have something to hold onto.

Autumn passed in a leafy whirl of mortification for Seth. The coach rarely played him. Chagrined, he finally quit the team. Life was not yet moving at normal speed through Karen, but the numbness of loss was going. It was over a year since Charley had died. There was enough restored feeling in her to absorb her son's pain and still experience her own: Sometimes she would hear a song of hers playing on the radio and wonder how she had ever been able to write it, where the music had come from, now that it was so completely gone.

She felt a terrible inertia. There was no place she wanted to go really, but Christmas was coming and she needed to jostle both Seth and herself into an acceptance that life went on, and with it, celebrations. There was a drawer full of brochures from places she and Charley had talked of vacationing one day, the one day that would never come for him. To make it more bearable, she chose the place where Charley would have been least likely to go.

"We're going to Bali for Christmas," she said to Seth, putting travel folders on the kitchen table.

"Why aren't we going to Vermont?"

"I'm tired of being cold," she said. She left out that she didn't want to be reminded of Christmas past, when they had usually gone skiing. Besides, she couldn't run the risk of anything happening to Seth. In truth, she'd felt relieved at the coach's bullying him out of his love for football. To Karen, the game equated with possible injury, as skiing did. Charley had broken a leg one holiday in Wilmington, Vermont, and the hospital had looked like a scene from *M.A.S.H.* Those who had come seeking exhilaration, relaxation, romance, were laid out like the war wounded, as doctors set their bones. Karen had always been strictly an *après-ski* person, reading or playing piano back at the lodge, using the valid excuse of not wanting to injure her musicianly hands to cover her terror of things she could not control.

Then, she had just been phobic about hurting herself. Now, every day she looked down apprehensively from her apartment window, watching Seth cross the street to catch the school bus as she had done when he was only eight. All of life had become about how fragile life was.

"Where's Bali?" he asked, without a real show of interest, his eyes on the sports pages, his voice overlaid with contained rage. Everything was changing: He'd lost his father; he'd lost his quarterbacking job. Now she was taking away what had always been their winter haven. The year before it had been too soon to think about going anywhere. At the time they were still walking into walls, glazed, going through the motions of continuing.

"It's in the Indian Ocean," she said. "An island in Indonesia."

"The place with the soldiers shooting students?"

"None of that happens in Bali. Bali has a life of its

own." She'd checked it out with the State Department, and although Americans were warned against going to Jakarta, there'd been no reports of danger in Bali.

"It's supposed to be . . ." She took out the articles she'd collected for years, all the time she'd been looking for ways to put the romance back in her marriage. What luxury women indulged themselves in, dreaming of ecstasy. ". . . the Last Paradise."

"Where's the first one?"

"Eden."

"I meant someplace real. Someplace closer. What's wrong with St. Bart's? A lot of my friends are going there."

"I feel like exploring," she said, not wanting to go anywhere she'd been with Charley, canceling out the therapeutic effect of a vacation with the pain of recollection. Nor did she care to risk running into anyone she knew, people whose eyes were shaded with pity, or shifting with uneasiness that she might need some help from them. It had been months since she'd been invited to the last of the sympathy lunches. The extra, unattached woman at a dinner party was the least-sought-after person in town. And as more time passed, when friends thought of you at all, they felt guilty at not having called, so didn't call. "Where's your sense of adventure?"

"I don't have any," he said, as his father had said in answer to the same, often-asked question. "I like what I know."

"How do you know you won't like what you don't know until you try it?"

"I just do," he said, stubbornly.

"Why don't you go over some of these brochures, and see what interests you. And you can plan some of the things we might enjoy doing together."

He looked up. "How far is it?"

It was so far that by the time they got there, he had become irate at how long the trip had taken, seen three movies, listened to several of the CDs he'd brought along, his portable player and the speakers set up on the floor in front of his seat, connecting headphones over his ears, and fallen into a deep sleep. She envied him his ability to take pleasure and solace from music. She herself had all but stopped listening to any, she felt so bereft at her lack of inspiration. As a token gesture she had brought along a small electronic keyboard, in the unlikely event that melody might come back to her. But she held little hope of that happening. Meanwhile, Seth slept with music leaking from his earphones, and a smile on his face.

He awakened having forgiven her. He seemed to have forgotten what it was he had been mad about, so relieved was he to arrive.

Outside the terminal, the air of Denpasar felt liquid against Karen's skin. Even motionless, it was like a caress, gentle fingers on her flesh. They had been in palm-treed places before, where the humidity was cloying. But there was a sweetness to the wetness here, texture that was almost a fragrance. The damp permeated her pores with the perfume of tropical flowers, moved through her nostrils, honeyed her tongue. She did not speak her feelings aloud to Seth, who sometimes appeared annoyed by her acute observations, wanting to make a few of his own.

"The air feels different," he said aloud, with a sense of discovery and pleasure.

She gave unspoken thanks. They were cut from the same cloth, connected by their sensibilities. Charley's gene pool had kicked in the broad-chested, thick-haired male plumage. But the subtleties were hers.

They took a taxi to the hotel, a place she'd booked through her travel agent, who'd described it as "modest but clean." The driver pulled up to the wood-carved statues that sided the portico.

"Eight million rupiah," he said to Karen, unloading the luggage as she and Seth got out of the cab.

"How much is that in dollars?" Karen asked, preparing to pay in her own currency.

"Thirty," said the driver.

"In your dreams," said a tall, dark-skinned man, tanned so deeply he might have seemed a native, were it not for his English accent and the vivid blue of his eyes. He was dressed in cut-offs and a tank top, which strained across his well-developed chest, arms muscular and athletic. He wore a soft white hat, pulled down so it completely covered his head.

Not until he took the hat off in a kind of sweeping, low bow to her did she see how sunbleached his hair was, how mischievous his expression. Then he leaned toward the driver and said a few words in what Karen assumed was the Bali language. The driver made a disappointed face.

"Eight dollars," the driver said reluctantly.

The Englishman smiled. "Well done," he said, seemingly as much to himself as the driver.

Sour-faced, the driver dumped the luggage abruptly on the grass and got back into his taxi, driving off. "No, really, it's perfectly all right," the Englishman called after the departing car, its tailpipe belching dark smoke. "We can manage on our own." He stood for a moment without speaking. "Rude bugger," he noted.

Seth looked at the stranger and then started picking up the cases. The Englishman leaned over to take one.

"No," Seth stopped him. "Like you said. We can manage on our own." His expression was steely. The Englishman shrugged, and walked away.

"Why were you so impolite to that man?" Karen asked Seth as she signed the register. "He was only trying to be helpful."

"Are you sure?" Seth said.

It bothered Karen that since his father's death Seth
often seemed wise beyond his years, a crustiness that had
hardened over his wound. In this case his reaction seemed
not so much wisdom as cynicism. But as the man meant
nothing to her, and Seth meant everything, she did not
dispute him.

A bellman brought a small trolley, loaded their bags
onto it, and led them toward their room. The hotel was
simple, Bali style, with open living rooms, an outdoor
shower for each accommodation, hanging elephant grass
thatched on the roof. The humidity was palpable, but there
were sliding doors the desk clerk advised could be pulled
closed, and, even in the half-open lobby, what passed for
air-conditioning. For some reason, Karen didn't mind the
heat. There was a light breeze. It moved through her body
like soft words, spoken in a man's voice.

The woman behind the reception desk had put garlands
around their necks. Karen was sotted with the heavy scent
of frangipani, a smell that usually would have been too
overpowering for her. But it went with the place. Sultry.
Mysterious. Sensual. Overdone.

"This really is a tropical island," Seth said, looking
around at the lush growth, red hibiscus, extruding yellow
pistils dusted with gold. A small, shallow pool in the courtyard leading to their room was thick with lotuses, white-
yellow in the afternoon, glinting with hints of the sunset to
come, pink at the edges. Coconut palms martialed the road

that lay outside the hotel, fronds hanging, weighed down by golden-shelled fruit.

"Unreal," Seth murmured, and so it seemed. Pyramids of bright orange marigolds, striped with fuchsia zinnias set on curled, coiled young coconut palm leaves, stood offered up in front of the tiny outdoor temple, a sanctuary for those who worked in the hotel. There were not many maids or clean-up people around the place that Karen could see, but those who did labor there had to have a temple or they wouldn't come to work because the place wasn't sacred. Spiritual life was the center of the Bali culture, so no one would take a job where they could not also pray. On the plane, Seth had read that fact to her from a guidebook, giving the information a slightly sardonic tone, imparting without saying aloud his appraisal of such orthodoxy, superstition, religion, whatever it was that made people defer to the invisible.

Still, he seemed to be losing his skepticism in the face of the beauty. The place was not much more than a motel, but it was hard to tell that with the exoticism of the surroundings, the feel of heaviness that was more than jet lag. It seemed to Karen she could intuit an almost supernatural power underfoot, the curious sensation that she was actually connected to the earth. Maybe it wasn't just almost. Maybe it *was* supernatural.

"All right!" Seth exclaimed, noting the clarity of the sky, the lushness of the foliage. And then "Thank you," he said, softly, resistance cracking like a shell, all the friends playing without him in St. Bart's, skiing without him in Vermont, forgotten. "Thanks, Mom."

Karen turned her head so he wouldn't see the relief. He wasn't mad at her anymore. Sometimes victory came not with winning, but having the battle disappear.

Seth was far ahead of her now, out of sight, following the bellman with his primitive trolley, trailbreaking his way toward their room. All at once Karen felt a different kind of heat from what hung on the air.

She could sense the man before she even saw him again. There was an aroma, a heavy male perfume. Then, there he was. Tanned so dark he might have been a native, except for his eyes. They moved to her, fixed on her. She felt flustered, off balance from her own reaction: a tug in her stomach as though someone had touched her from inside.

His face was ruggedly handsome, with angular cheekbones and an imposing nose. She felt suddenly like a teenager, even as she judged herself silly, giddy, reminding herself how old she she was.

"Thank you for your help before," she said as she went past him, quickening her step.

"Only the beginning," he said. Angled slightly backward, just a touch atilt, he seemed to be looking down at her. He reminded her of the naughty boys she had been drawn to in her adolescence, the kind who kissed and ran away.

She was suddenly awash in his scent, Drakkar, a men's cologne she sometimes sniffed at the counters of department stores to quiet her loneliness, a fragrance she had once given Charley, which he'd rarely worn and left in a hotel room on vacation. Mixed with the sweet smell of frangipani around her neck, it affected her like a narcotic. She nearly stumbled. The man saw.

"Bali magic," he said, his look amused, as though he were reading what was going on inside her.

"I beg your pardon?"

"Everything comes into your life that's supposed to, just at the moment it should." There was a jagged scar to the left of the center of his upper lip, slightly constricting his smile.

The imperfection stirred her. She had a sudden wish to touch him, to finger the scar. She was surprised at the force of the impulse.

Musical bells sounded in the near distance. She heard them clearly, resonating in a part of her head that she thought had been numbed forever, marked where the notes would fall on a more familiar Western musical scale. The man held her eyes in what felt like a grip, turning it into an exploration.

His teeth, very white against his skin, had no points to them, a curious square uniformity. She guessed he was in his early thirties. There was a gold ring on his sunbrowned right hand, some kind of school ring it seemed. Around his neck hung a piece of money, an old Bali coin, a hole through its center, strung with black leather. "How long are you here for?" he asked.

"Two weeks," she said.

"Not a lot of time." Truth sounded through the words, along with flirtation, as if he knew, young as he was, how speedily it all went. "Of course time is different in Bali. Days seem to go on forever. If I can be of service . . ."

He handed her a card. It was a very formal gesture for such an open, natural, Third World place. She could feel the temperature of his skin across the short distance separating them, a quick spark of electricity between their fingertips. His hands were big, weather coarsened, but with clean, filed nails. She took the card as briskly as if contact with his flesh might burn her.

It read "Richard Hensley." Underneath the name was a phone number, and the printed legend "Tour Guide– Surfing Instruction– Hiking– White-Water Rafting." A line was drawn through the last.

"Well, thank you. Maybe I'll be in touch."

"Oh, I would hope so. Days that seem endless need to be filled."

She felt actually young, caught in a tangle of old feelings. She stood awkwardly. It took a physical effort for her to resume walking, and she did it at a faster pace.

He fell into step beside her, holding out his hand. "As it reads on the card, Richard Hensley."

"You're English." She ignored his extended hand, not meaning to be discourteous as much as afraid to touch him.

"British, used to be. But we've given all that up. The empire, you know. And you are . . ."

He waited for her name. "Here with my son," she said, and kept walking.

Two

"THERE'S WHERE the bells are coming from," Seth said when she had caught up with him, pointing to some musicians on the sand. Suddenly eager, Seth was pulling her by the hand, in the open way he hadn't since declaring himself finished with childhood. "Let's change into bathing suits and go down to the beach."

Behind her she could hear the soft padding of the sandaled feet of the Englishman. He was whistling, a wind contrast to the metallic bells, counterpointing with melody what the musicians were playing. It started to form a kind of song in her head.

The bellman, a fragile older man who pushed their bags on a dolly, unlocked their room. Seth helped him carry the luggage inside.

Just before she went through the door, Karen half-turned. The young Englishman was walking around a stone statue, an elephant head on a sitting man's pot-bellied body.

"Ganesha." He pointed to it. "The god of Overcoming all Obstacles."

She narrowed her eyes a little against the glare of the day, the unexpected dazzle of the Brit. Like his aroma, there seemed to be an aura around him: charm, the splendor of the day, youth, all of it combining to cast a kind of spell on her, so that her vision appeared slightly blurred. Or maybe her eyes were just getting older, or the trip had wearied her more than she knew. She started inside.

"And so we shall," Richard Hensley called out.

"Why were you talking to that guy back there?" Seth asked after the bellman had gone. "That Englishman. Who is he?"

"He's a tour guide."

"I don't need a tour guide. I'm going to figure this place out for myself." He started rummaging in his suitcase for a bathing suit.

"They talk about how the sea sparkles, but I never really saw it before," Seth said, as they stood on the grass that led down to the ocean. "It must be the angle of the sun, below the equator and all that."

He observed the Indian Ocean for a moment as Homer might have, had he been on that side of the world, arms ruggedly crossed, lending weight to his contemplation. Then he charged into the water, handing her his towel.

Karen rented a chair from a man who had a thatched-grass concession stand under an umbrella. She moved the chair beneath a row of palm trees, monitoring Seth's splashes, holding an open book on her lap so it wouldn't look as though she were watching him. The tropics had not been a big part of their history. So the ocean, with Seth swimming in it, made her uneasy.

"May I join you?" Richard Hensley said, not waiting for an answer, easing himself onto the sand beside her, his smile warm, friendly, his eyes interested. His voice had a slightly metallic edge to it, the gently cutting timbre of aristocratic Brits, who always sounded as if they were about to deflate hot air, or add to it.

It was a tone that augured wit. "If you like."

"Oh, I do. I like very much." He stretched out his well-muscled brown legs, the sparse, silky-looking hairs on them bleached gold. "Isn't it funny how you just know about some people, instantly?"

"Know what?"

"How easy they are to be around. Old soul kind of thing, like you've been with each other before."

"Oh, I haven't been with you," she said. "I would have

remembered." She sat up straighter and looked at the ocean where Seth had been, giving herself over to the role of vigilant mother. The surf made rhythmic, lapping noises. The wind stroked her neck with moist fingers.

Seth popped up from beneath the water. He waved at her. She returned his wave. He grinned, confidence fortified, then dove back under.

"Is that the heir?" Richard asked.

"It is."

"Looks like a fine, healthy fellow. Maybe I can take you both on an excursion."

"He doesn't want a tour guide. He wants to discover Bali for himself."

"Well, good for him if he can do it." Richard lay back, arms behind his head. "This is a place filled with difficulty. Mystery. People think they're having a tropical vacation. But it's a mirror, where you learn about your own soul. If you want to go that deep."

"Do you?"

"It was not my original intention. But when you're here long enough, you have no choice." The jagged pink scar pulled a little on his lip.

Once again, she suppressed the impulse to reach and touch it. "How long have you been here?"

"Ten years," he said.

An undertone of melancholy tempered the brashness, giving him dimension, sorrow, loss. "You must have been a boy."

"Still am," Richard said, eyes shifting back to her. Art-fulness closed back over the honesty, like shutters.

"So it's perfect for you here, then. You can play."

"Not all the time. Sometimes I'm dead serious." His look became suggestive, provocative.

"Is that what you do, besides being a guide? Prey on older women?"

"Oh," he said, his smile rakish. "Are you older?"

There was the scent of blossoms in the air, the salty fragrance of the sea, meat cooking on the grill of an open restaurant. The sun glinted off the water, slanted through the palm fronds, played on their skin. Karen tried to con-centrate on her book. She could feel Richard's attention on her, sense him over the other strong aromas, heat intensify-ing his smell, mixing the pleasantly heavy scent of Drakkar with the slight saltiness of his perspiration.

She felt woozy. Jet-lagged, she supposed. But along with the lightheadedness were her emotions, flailing about, unloosed. Her reason informed her he was not to be trusted, that people should be known before you trusted. But what she was starting to feel had nothing to do with reason. "What time is it?" she asked him, trying to sober herself with the mundane, a pinch of reality to rouse her from dreaming.

"Well, there's no real linear time here," he said. "Like

when you have to be someplace, or you're trying to do things. There's soul time. Body time. You can be in a temple for a half hour or a day, and you can't tell the difference. When I said the days go on forever, it's because they really seem to. Time doesn't happen at one time, but all time is happening. We live our pasts in the present."

"Still, you *do* have a watch," she said, smiling.

He looked at it. "It's Now," he said.

"The past is a memory, and the future is a fantasy?" she said.

"I knew it!" He sat up sharply, looked at her with intensified interest. "I said to myself, even as I wanted you on the basest of levels, I said, that woman is *aware*. She *knows*."

Like a clarion call came the announcement of his attraction. The basest of levels. Wanting her. She felt actually giddy.

"Knows what?" Seth said, at the foot of the chair suddenly, up from the sea like a water sprite, dripping, his usually unruly hair flat against his skull.

"Spiritual truths. Some aspects of Buddhism," Richard said, getting to his feet. "Living in the moment, and all that." He held out his hand. "Richard Hensley."

Seth shook it halfheartedly, giving his own name, measuring the man with his eyes. They were about the same height, but the Englishman looked a little taller, making Seth pull himself up to his full measure. He stretched, the veins in his neck visible. "You some kind of missionary?"

"I guess you could say that." Richard picked up the towel Karen held and handed it to the boy.

Seth eyed it suspiciously before taking it, as if not sure he wanted to accept even a small courtesy from this man. He wrapped it around himself, his eyes wary beneath matted lashes. "I'm surprised a preacher can afford a vacation in Bali."

"I'm not on vacation," said Richard. "And I'm not exactly a preacher."

"What exactly are you?"

"A tour guide."

"I had four guys try to sell me watches between here and the ocean," Seth said. "Are you selling something?"

"Only the spirit of Bali," said Richard, smiling pleasantly. "The pleasures of life."

"Pay no attention to the man behind the green curtain," Seth said.

"I beg your pardon?"

"The snake-oil guy in *The Wizard of Oz,* who fakes that he's the wizard, and when he's caught behind the green curtain he says, 'Pay no attention to the man behind the green curtain.' "

"Well, I don't claim to be a wizard. And I don't sell snake oil."

"But you are . . ." He seemed to grope the air for just the right word. ". . . an opportunist?"

"Seth!"

"I don't mind," Richard said. "Not such a bad thing to

be. *Carpe diem*. Seize the day. We ought all to be opportunists or we might never catch our opportunity when it appears."

"Well, yours isn't here," Seth said, and held out his hand for Karen. "Come on."

"I'm so sorry," Richard said. "I thought you were her son. I didn't realize you were her husband."

"Sometimes I wonder who raised you," Karen said, back in the room.

"That guy is no good."

"You don't know that. You shouldn't have called him an opportunist."

"Well, how do they say it where he comes from? Wastrel?"

"Why do you jump to these conclusions?"

"It's pretty clear. Aren't you even excited I knew that word? Cool, huh? 'Wastrel.' " He roostered around the room for a minute. "You're a pushover for charm."

"Don't leave out good looks."

"I don't think he's that good-looking."

"I was talking about you." She walked into the bathroom, put the plug in the small, square tub, slightly deeper than a footbath, and turned the faucets on.

He was close behind her, checking himself out in the mirror, flexing his pecs. He seemed pleased.

"Good looks are no substitute for manners," she said.

"He's just so obvious." Seth picked up his shampoo, examining it as though it held his full attention, and what he said was offhand. "And you're a real target."

"Since when did you become such a judge of character?"

"It comes with being a man of the world," Seth said. "You were the one who wanted me to travel."

She worried about him, as she usually worried, but this was worry of a new and different kind: When had he started being so suspicious of people? Was this, too, a side effect of losing his father, a sudden outcrop of skepticism about everybody? Or was it not everybody, but just this man?

Sunset was a celebration in Bali. Young children on small, flat wooden boards rode the foam at the water's edge. Some surfed the shallows on their bellies, dark little dots against the pinks and violets trailing the sinking of the sun, reflected on the tide-silvered sand. On the terraces of the many hotels along that stretch of beach guests gathered, colorful cocktails in hand, observing the ritual. Like an obedient student, Karen followed the suggestion of the circular someone had handed them at the airport, not to miss sunset, while Seth, still upside down in time, took a nap.

"They're different every sunset," Richard Hensley said,

all at once behind her, his voice little more than a whisper, like wind, rustling the hair on the back of her neck. "Blazing sometimes, bright orange. Or lavender on days like this, where there're cloud streams low on the horizon."

He had changed into pressed chinos and a ruffled white shirt. He looked almost dressed for a party. She could feel the temperature of his skin from that little distance away. She felt charged, electric.

The hair that had swung matted from underneath his cap was now slicked back, sides shiny against his well-shaped head. She would have liked to loosen it, make it come undone.

A glint of orange appeared below the clouds, just above the horizon, the last slim disk of sun, sinking in the water.

"In a few minutes, after it sets, if you stand on the beach," he said, "you can see the whole sky illuminated. Streaks all across it, because of where we are, below the equator. There's a ring of dust in the upper atmosphere, reflecting the ghost of the light. It completely renews you."

"You think I need renewal?"

"Everybody does," said Richard. "Fortunately, the cells in our bodies change completely every seven years. So we can start afresh. How long have you been divorced?"

"I'm a widow."

"I'm sorry. . . ." He paused, caught himself. "No, that isn't true. I *am* sorry you had to go through that. But I'm glad you're alone."

"Are you?" she asked.

"Come," he said, offering his hand. "You must experience this to the full."

Gingerly, she let her fingertips be taken in his. She could feel a perceptible tingle. His hand closed gently around hers, thumb slipping past the curve of her index finger, into the hollow of her palm. A rush of sensation, velvety, hot, puddled in the center. He led her down to the beach. Her breath came in starts, as though she'd been running.

He took her by the elbow, the kind of touch that appeared polite, making sure she wouldn't stumble. But his skin was on her skin, so what she experienced had little to do with good manners.

"Can you feel it?" They stood on the sand watching colors change, the luminous trail of streaks in the sky, shining white, silver, purple.

"What?"

"How endless the day is."

She felt more than that.

"And how come *you're* alone?" she asked him, echoing his question to her as they walked on the beach.

"It's the decent thing to be. When I'm with people I usually hurt them."

"You're trying to scare me," she said.

"I'm trying to warn you," he insisted, even as his skin brushed hers.

"You want to seem dangerous."

"And do I?"

"You do to my son," she said.

"He's a bit sophisticated for a boy his age," Richard said.

"He's always seemed older than he is. Very verbal. Clever. But he's gotten edgier since he lost his dad."

"And very protective of you," Richard noted.

"You think that's good?"

"Probably for you. I'm not sure about me."

They continued along the beach. She could see his fine profile in the afterlight and wondered about him, and women. "Don't you get lonely?" she said.

"Everyone gets lonely. Even people surrounded by people get lonely."

It was true. "But what about . . ." Longings, she wanted to say. But the word seemed too sentimental for men. "Tender feelings?"

He half-smiled, the scar on his lip pulling at his mouth. He didn't answer.

"You're being mysterious."

"Am I?"

"Yes. It's part of trying to seem dangerous."

"What exactly do you mean by dangerous?"

"Someone who can break your heart."

"Then don't involve your heart."

"I don't know how not to."

"I'll teach you," he said. "I'll be your tour guide." He touched the inside of her wrist, pulled her close enough so that she could feel the warmth of his well-toned belly through his shirt. It was not that bold a gesture: The pull had seemed almost incidental. But it jolted her.

She was moved in places she'd forgotten were in her body. Not just the sensuality of it, but the lightness of his touch, the temperature of his skin aroused her. It was the accumulated ache, the absence of contact, the tactile reminder she was flesh. The full rush of the passion she'd had years to express but hadn't expressed to the full, never realizing how ephemeral the chance for passion was. She had been sure that chance was over. And yet—here it was again.

He moved closer. It was growing dark. Where they were standing on the sand no torches were lighted. She could barely make out his features. But she could see, even in the shadows, the shape of his mouth as he wet his lips, the scar. She longed to touch it.

"What are you thinking?" he asked her.

"I would like . . ." She stopped herself. Why? Why be reluctant to say? Life went by so quickly, irredeemable. What was she saving herself for? It wasn't as though she were still a girl. "I'd like you to kiss me."

"Oh, I intend to kiss you," he said, and leaned away from her. Maddening her. A *very* dangerous man.

The beach was lit now with torches, streams of light from a waxing moon. "What brought you to Bali?" she said.

"Disgrace."

Karen did not ask what, exactly, constituted the disgrace. The word itself seemed sadly straightforward, self-negating, his own severed head held out on a tray. What she had felt at the sight of the wound on his mouth intensified, merged with her instincts to nurture, to make things better, to soothe. Their bodies brushed as they walked, her bare arms whisked by the fabric of his shirt. Fixed on the tightness of his damaged mouth, she wondered what it would taste like.

From the terrace of the hotel, above the dunes, came the bell-like sound of music, the repetitious rhythms of Bali, a kind of melodic mantra, the same phrase over and over again, till a tense Westerner's teeth were set on edge, or the mind got clear. She tried to give herself over to the cadence, and started to hear it as a professional would, began to lose herself in the music. But not completely. She was too conscious of the big presence beside her, painfully aware of her own growing desire, chagrined by the realization she had that much hunger in her. So quickly.

"And you?" he said. "What brought you to Bali?"

"I wanted to go somewhere I'd never been with . . ."

"Don't say his name," said Richard.

"Why?"

"I don't want to know that much about him. I don't want him to be real."

The sand grew suddenly wet beneath her bare feet, a rivulet of fresh water coming from the land above, toward the sea, making its own rushing stream. She had left her sandals near the hotel stairs, and the sudden cold on her instep surprised her. She gave a little start. He reached for her arm, steadied her. She could feel the temperature of his blood through his skin, the shape of his fingers, thick, blunt, square at the tops of his nails.

She wondered if the elbow he held onto was soft enough, if she'd creamed it sufficiently over the years. She wondered if the breasts that (don't say his name) had prized so were still sufficiently high in their fullness to arouse this man, as his merely being at her side, his fingertips on her flesh, were arousing her. Was she really that foolish, that vulnerable? Or might it not be a gift? Couldn't it be what he had said in the courtyard? Bali magic?

There were whispers of wind along the embankment, like softest sighs. She could almost feel spirits dancing around her. Maybe there were. Maybe she was being invaded by benign demons, the dark deities whose statues were everywhere in Bali, the ones with wicked masks that no one seemed frightened of, not even children. Every statue was draped from the waist down with black and white checkered cloth: Good and evil, it said in the guide book; Yin and Yang. You couldn't have the light without the dark side. And if for her the dark side was her own sensuality, perhaps it was time it emerged. Fully. Everything didn't have to be consecrated, holy. Maybe the invisible force that gave the island its purported power was robbing her of will, restraint. Maybe she could behave like a fool and blame it on the spirits.

She and Richard walked for a while, past terraces filled with chatter and laughter, music drifting from patios, the smell of cooking food. Exhaustion, the change in time, closeness, the denial since her widowing, the desire Karen tried not to show, all combined. She felt suspended in time, in the time Richard had told her was no longer time as she knew it. She believed him. It was as though she had known him, perhaps not in previous lives, but a strangely long time in this one. From the corner of her eye, in the moonlight, she could see the proud tip of his nose, pointing like an arrow to that damaged mouth.

"What happened to your mouth?" she asked him.

"I fell on my face a few times," he said. "Woke up in a pool of blood now and then. They had to sew me back together."

Irresistible. Danger and a need for rescue combined.

"I don't think I can wait much longer," she said.

"For what?"

"For you to kiss me."

He stopped, looked at her for a moment, and then swooped in at her, hard, surprisingly inept, the kiss of an amateur. She had imagined from how good-looking he was, and how charming he had seemed from the start, plus his air of mystery, his perfect qualifications for rogue, that he would have been more practised. But his lips were solid, firm, resistant against hers, no pliancy to them, no expertise.

Still there was a sweet taste to his mouth, clove, piquant and strong. It moved across her tongue as his tongue did, sucked her deeper into feeling, gave the fleshly exchange the extra dimension of flavor, as if this were more than a doorway to making love. She could imagine feasting on him.

"Your lips are so strong," she said, covering her disappointment at the surprising inflexibility of his mouth with what seemed like praise. "It's like they have muscles in them. Have you been working out?"

"Not my mouth," he said. "My mouth hardly at all."

"Then let me exercise it for you." She hadn't realized fully till his mouth touched hers, blundering though the contact was, how much she had longed for another mouth. More than technique, more than sex. Lips to kiss her back, to alleviate the loneliness.

She took his face between her hands, gently eased it a little away, softened the kiss, sipped his lips, drinking her way across. It felt like a healing. She moved her face into the hollow of his throat, smelled his skin, the heavy aroma, like incense now with the smoky cooking scents coming from the restaurants, the wind through the night-blooming flowers, the salt of the sea. She strained for the sound of his breath, the taste of it, sweet, pungent, moist.

Taking his hint from her, he moved his lips onto her collarbone, kissed his way up her neck to her ear, touched the tip of his tongue to the back of her lobe, circled it. She sighed from a place deeper than her throat.

"Come back with me to my place," Richard said.

"Not now," she said. "It's too soon." Not just the residue of the good girl she had been in her youth stopped her, but the warning she had gotten from her son. How did she know who this man was, really? It was not a time in sexual history to be flippant about making love, nor was it time in her personal history, seriously as she took things. Not yet anyway. Not till the wind and the music and his touch combined to stir her completely.

She turned back in the direction of her hotel, ignoring Richard's look of annoyance. Reluctantly, he fell into step beside her. As they walked, the irritation seemed to leave him, like a boy who'd lost a round of a game but, after a brief flare of temper, resumed playing. He put his arm around her.

She'd forgotten the feel of that as well: the casual protection of a tall man's arm, like a shield against the wind, which, even balmy as it was, ruffled. She remembered how sustaining that action had felt when Charley did it, the seemingly careless way he had of being careful with her.

Richard's hand slipped towards her breast. "Don't," she said. "Please."

"How long has it been?"

"Not long enough."

"Nonsense. If he loved you, and he must have, he wouldn't have wanted you to be alone. Not with all the life you have in you. You owe it to yourself to live fully. You're a passionate woman."

"Who mustn't let the passion get out of hand."

"Why not? That's what makes it passion. The strongest force on the planet. The reason we're all here."

"You think the goal of life is passion?"

"I didn't mean the goal. I meant the *source*. If it weren't for passion, we'd none of us have been born." He was touching her arm now, in an insinuating way, working his fingers along the soft flesh of the inside.

"I came here for my son," she said, remembering the brochures she had tried to charm him with, the plans she had suggested he make of things he might like to do. "This holiday was for him. He's already jealous of you."

"Highly territorial, boys are."

"I worry about him."

"Then I shall worry about him, too," he said, congeniality returning to his tone. "I shall win him. You'll see. I'll charm the little bugger."

"I woke up and you weren't here," Seth said when she got back to the room. "You weren't here and I wasn't sure where I was. Then when I knew where I was I still didn't know where anything was, like the restaurant or anything."

His face was lined with sleep, the impressions of the creases in the pillow on it. He looked dazed, cherubic, heartbreakingly young.

"Would you like to go get some dinner? Are you hungry?"

"Not anymore. I ate about twenty of those little bananas in the fruit bowl. They look like fingers. I felt like a cannibal."

"Can you go to sleep again? If we go to sleep now, we can maybe wake up when it's their morning."

"Where were you?"

"Walking on the beach."

"With that guy?"

"I don't think I have to report to you."

"Why can't you just say 'Yes,'" Seth said. "Are you ashamed that you were with him?"

"Why should I be ashamed?"

"You're older than he is."

"Not that much."

"He acts young enough to be your son."

"*You're* young enough to be my son," she said, and went into the bathroom.

She slept fitfully, muddled by the difference in time, unsettled by her reawakened sexual feelings, anxious at Seth's reaction. The whole reason for the trip had been to alleviate tension between them, not cause it. The relationship was so complex, mother–son: longing for connection, fear that the connection might be too close, even without the death of a father, even if there'd never been Freud. She'd wanted to use this time to get close to Seth, in the healthiest possible way, not to confront him with a rival.

Still, she had forgotten how it felt to be smitten. And she was. Old to be Juliet. It had taken a lot of strength to resist Richard. Even as he fumed, considering her constraint foolish, she silently agreed with him, wondering why she could not be foolish enough, foolish faster. Before she'd left on this trip, she'd gone for her yearly physical, and her doctor had asked, as he asked all women patients, if she was sexually active. The question had made her weep because she missed Charley so, longed for the passion that had been between them.

So it was exciting to hold her breath again, not out of fear, or grief, but anticipation. To wait for a touch, like a longed-for letter, and have it delivered. Fumblingly perhaps, but still welcome, still arousing. Even as she dozed, half-sleeping, she responded to the memory of his touch, the kiss begun so awkwardly, which had become the kiss she engineered and hadn't realized she so desperately wanted. Not just what he gave, but all she put into it. All she wanted to put into it, everything stored up in her, longing to burst free.

"Get away!" Seth shouted in his sleep.

It shocked her into wakefulness like a reprimand. Karen turned on the light by her bed, checked the room for monsters, the demons of childhood that still pursued him. His face on the pillow was strained with rage, the reflex that came from fear.

What was he afraid of? What was he *not* afraid of, now that he knew how capricious life was? How tenuous. How ready to Indian-give all sense of security. Not politically correct, she supposed. Native American–give, it would have to be altered to, even within the confines of the brain, so that memory would not seem bigoted.

How much the world had changed, becoming oversensitive but no better. Only love had stayed the same, unaltered, for the soft in heart. Soft in head, she amended. Vulnerable in body. Desire, coming in a rush, with no respect for age, and apparently no regard for experience.

It was as though her years had been lobotomized. Everything she'd learned in her long, rich relationship with Charley—not always rich with good, but unremittingly interesting—had been brushed away like cobwebs with the brash young Englishman's broom. She was young again, ignorant, naive, as much as she tried to seem in control. The feel of heat beneath his skin, the skin itself, his smell, the pleasantly looming presence had ricocheted her back into girlhood. "At your age, Madam," Hamlet had said to his mother, "the fire in the blood is tame." Shakespeare might have known more than anyone before or since about drama, comedy, and words, but he knew precious little about women.

"Why is the light on?" Seth asked crankily.

"You were talking in your sleep," she said.

"I'm sorry. Did I wake you up?"

"I wasn't really sleeping."

"What time is it in the regular world?"

"If we think in those terms, we'll never get comfortable the whole time we're in Bali."

He sat up. "I feel very much at home here."

"Good."

"Not necessarily," he said. "I haven't felt that comfortable for a while at home."

He saw the anguish on her face. "I was only joking. I know how much you've done to try and make sure I was happy."

"And are you?"

"Now and then," he said. "Are you?"

"I will be."

"When?"

"When we stop fencing and can be with each other again the way we were before."

"That's over," he said. "Dad isn't coming back."

"I know that."

"So how can it ever be the way it was? Am I supposed to be having a good time? You drag me halfway around the world, away from my friends, and then leave me to hang out with that beach bum."

"Why do you call him that? What do you know about him?"

"It's just my initiation," Seth said.

"I think you mean intuition."

"Whatever it is, it's sharper than yours."

"Maybe," she said. "Maybe it is." Was it? Richard had noted that Seth was sophisticated for his age. Was he even more sophisticated than his mother? She seemed to have been stripped of her years, flung back into girlhood.

She walked over to the dresser where she'd put her portable electronic keyboard, and switched it on. Struck a note. A few of them. The sounds she had heard echoing on the beach, now resonating in her head. The part of her brain that she thought had died, coming back to life. As the rest of her was.

"And then again," he said kindly, "maybe he's not really a bad guy, your Buddhist."

"He's not a Buddhist. And he isn't mine."

"But I am," Seth said, his voice cracking, unsure, strained by an apparent underpinning of fear that perhaps someone else had jumped his claim. "I am, really."

"Yes, you are," she said, and got up, went to the folding bed where he leaned on one elbow, and held him. "Yes, you are."

Three

TINY BIRDS with rounded white heads and golden bills flitted above their heads, hovering like humming-birds, in cheerful flight to nowhere in particular. Breakfast tables at a restaurant on the beach were shaded by oversized, vividly colored umbrellas, red and purple and gold, with bright yellow fringes, splashes of man-made brilliance against the glittering turquoise of the sea, the mica-shiny beige of the sands, the lustrous, dark green of frangipani leaves and palm fronds.

Already the sun was too strong to face directly. Tourists who had apparently pledged themselves a morning consti-tutional had finished their long walks on the beach by eight o'clock, when tide and surf were low, the air still tinged with silver. Only the hardiest of plants seemed to stand up squarely to the glare; even the most obviously committed vacationers wore hats. But Seth sat bareheaded, his thick yellow curls cascading around his red-tipped ears.

"You better move into the shade," Karen suggested. She was sure he had to feel uncomfortable but was unwilling to show anything that seemed the least like weakness.

"Okay," he said grudgingly, and changed his chair.

The table was bright with tropical fruits, cut at artful angles, a presentation. At the next table a family of Australians ate scrambled eggs with caviar, the father spooning it into his toddler's mouth.

"You don't think that's too rich for her?" the mother asked.

"It's part of the package," the father said, and kept on feeding.

At a table facing Karen, a pair of young lovers nibbled at fruit-covered pancakes, and each other's fingers. The young man tilted his head towards the woman, touched crowns, licked the syrup from the corners of her mouth, segued into a kiss.

Seeing his mother's face, Seth turned to see what so held her attention. "Mush," he muttered.

"It isn't nice to stare," Karen said.

"Then you better stop," said Seth, and returned his gaze to his own plate.

But focused as Karen tried to be on her food, her eyes would wander, from the face of her son, and the sea behind him, to the lovers, and their interaction. She could feel a twinge, an emptiness between the pit of her belly and her genitals. The young man's hand moved down the woman's half-bare chest to the hollow between her breasts, pressed tightly by her sarong. He slipped his finger inside the fabric and touched her nipple, making it harden, evident through the cloth.

Karen looked away, poured herself a second cup of coffee, reached into a porcelain bowl, took out a bright yellow packet. Seth stopped her hand.

"Life is short," he said. "Don't use artificial sweeteners."

Still, he was ready to be fearless about himself. He was determined to go exploring after breakfast, undeterred by Karen's misgivings, her anxiety that he would get lost, be harmed. "I won't take anything with me worth stealing," he assured her back in their room, taking off his watch, putting it under his mattress, going to a rickety chest of drawers for the miniature compass she had bought him in the airport at Singapore. "And there are no more tigers in Bali."

"But there *are* wild boars."

"Better than civilized ones," he said, and chortled. "Not bad, huh? What do you think? Am I as witty as Dad?"

"Every bit."

"Really?" The confident adventurer vanished, the child

returned, a need for approval in the hazel eyes. "You really think so? He *was* a pretty funny guy."

"So are you."

"The apple doesn't fall far from the tree, right?"

"Right."

"But maybe here . . ." He took some fruit from a bowl and put it into his bookbag with a bottle of water for his excursion. ". . . we should say the pineapple."

He seemed delighted with the pun, and she delighted with him. The sophistication that she feared was so out of place when it attached to something negative, like his doubts and suspicions about Richard, was endearing when he used it with a sense of play. But even as she rejoiced in him, it intensified anxieties about his welfare.

"I don't think you ought to go off on your own."

"You said there was no trouble on Bali," Seth said, half recapping, half accusatory. "It's only in Jakarta, and East Timor, and the other islands. Would you take the chance of bringing me here if there was really danger?"

"Of course not."

"So wasn't what you told me the truth?"

"Well, yes, but . . ."

"I'm not a kid," he said, desperation, uncertainty, hope, all combining in the assertion. "Either you have confidence in me, or get a baby sitter." He was standing very tall, looking very stubborn, heartbreakingly like his father.

"Be sure and use plenty of sunblock," she said.

On the far side of the crowded swimming pool, the amorous couple shared a single chaise. The man trailed his fingers slowly over the naked upper spine of the woman, reached for the glass that lay shaded beneath a table beside them. Taking an ice cube, he dipped it into the hollows at the backs of her knees, drew it upward over her thighs, made little semicircles on the exposed skin beneath her buttocks. From Karen's vantage point under an umbrella, her eyes concealed by opaque dark glasses, her book held as though she were actually reading it, she could follow every gesture. Almost feel it.

"Well, there you are, you pretty thing," said Richard Hensley, pulling up a chair. He was in his cutoffs, a tank top showing to full, darkly tanned advantage the strong definition in his arms, his forearms even more muscular than his shoulders and upper arms were. He looked around, checked the swimmers in the pool. "Where's the dragon?"

"Gone exploring."

"It's pretty tame around here." He sat down. "I should take him into the mountains, give him a taste of real adventure."

"No, thank you," Karen said.

"If my mother had kept me on as tight a lead as you keep him . . ." His bright blue eyes were only slightly shaded by the brim of his straw hat. He half-squinted at her. ". . . I should never have become a man."

"To the great loss of women."

He smiled. "You think it's wrong that I love women?"

"All women?" She was filled with curiosity about him that was more than general curiosity. In America you asked what a man did, as a comfortable index to him, taking your time about trying to understand what he *was*. More often than not, in the case of women, they preferred not to really know too quickly what a man was if the answer might be disappointing: weak, a scoundrel, a cad. All of these thoughts flashed quickly through Karen's mind; she instantly dismissed them. She was no less guilty than her sisters about not wanting to hear bad news, especially when it involved a man to whom she was suddenly, deeply attracted.

After the time and anguish of being so alone, considering herself resigned to never having love again, Richard had come as a heart-lifting surprise. A tinge of obsession with him had already touched her, along with feelings that had fallen into limbo. She was curious about him and other women. Her own thoughts felt sinful, really, her widowhood having backed her into a prudish corner. But Richard was dazzling, the air was palpable on her skin, a soft breeze moving it into a kind of stroking.

"Not all women. Just the ones I've known."

She wondered how many there had been. "Men who love a great many women can't necessarily love one."

"Of course we can. One at a time." He looked at her with a gaze so compelling that even as he alluded to his philandering, she felt like the only woman in the world.

She bit her tongue so she wouldn't ask about the others. "Where did you go to school?" A good neutral question, one that had always worked at proms, on blind dates, both of which she had the feeling she was once again a part of, flung back in time to a naïveté her good sense would have judged appalling, if her good sense had been in play, rather than her senses.

"Uppingham," he said, "slightly upmarket from Eton and Harrow, though we don't get near the publicity." He signaled a man with a bar cart, who waved in return but made no sign of moving toward them. "These people do everything at their own pace." Irritation edged Richard's words. "It doesn't matter how long you've lived here, if you have a Western tempo, it could drive you mad."

"And has it?"

"Quite. But you can't show your anger, or they disappear. I have friends, expats who've built houses here. Made the mistake of showing their exasperation at the slowness of the workers. The crew simply went home at the end of the day and never came back."

"They don't care about money?"

"Oh, they like it. But they *love* harmony. It's part of their religion, you see. They're a sect of Hindu that believes in instant Karma. What you send out comes back immediately. So they're gallingly pleasant. They don't dare show anger for fear it will come back at them. And they believe in animism. Forces. Powers. That everything has a spirit. That's why they constantly make offerings to everything. Nature. The trees. Statues."

On her arrival she had noted the brilliantly decorated pyramid of fruit and flowers at the entrance to the hotel, considering it simply a local decoration. She realized now it must have been an offering to the place itself, so that the gods would give the guests a happy holiday. The thought enchanted her. "I like the sound of that," she said.

"I like the smell of you." He leaned forward in his chair until he was quite close to her, and closed his eyes, breathed in, deeply. "Vanilla, isn't it? Smell is a very important part of sexual attraction."

"Is it?" she asked, as if she didn't know, as if his smell wasn't becoming a hypnotic. The ability even to pretend indifference was a new talent for her. She had always been direct, too direct perhaps, totally open. Charley had often said that what was on her mind was on her tongue.

But this was Asia. People were supposed to have mystery. As far as she knew—and Seth was already convinced—Richard might have been full of duplicity. She struggled to be careful.

"May I offer you something?" the barman said, there, finally, leaning over Richard.

"What do you have that breaks down the will?" Richard asked.

"Pardon?"

"My son says there's no place for irony in the Bali language," Karen said.

"Right," Richard said. "I'll have a Singapore Sling," he told the barman, enunciating clearly. "And what will you have, Beauty?" He said it as if it were her name.

It touched her. Besides the flattery, it sounded affectionate. She dulled the part of her brain that considered perhaps he didn't remember at the moment what her name actually was. "It's a little early in the day for me."

"It's last night where you come from. Consider it a nightcap."

"I don't drink before I go to bed."

"What do you do before you go to bed?" he asked, with a wink in it. "What do you do when you're awake?"

"I'm a songwriter," she said. "Or at least I was."

"Will you sing me something you've written?"

"Did you want to order?" asked the barman, only his words a bit of a prod, his attitude nothing but patient.

"A Singapore Sling for Madame," Richard said. The barman moved away.

"A Singapore Sling. How exotic."

"Not in Bali. Singapore's just a hop away. 'Exotic' means from another part of the world. Striking. Unfamiliar."

"I didn't know that," Karen said.

He reached over and touched her lips, traced along the outside, moved the tip of his index finger between them. "You're exotic," he said.

"Well, Richard!" said a puff-bellied, balding man with an English accent, pulling himself up out of the pool, his gut hanging over the edge of his wet bathing suit. "I'd heard you were in this part of the world. Thought it was Singapore."

"Not for a long time," Richard said, looking less than pleased.

"Lord Hensley sent a letter to the presidents of all our Asian bank branches not to lend you money under any circumstances, so I imagined you'd be stuck there. Wondered why I never ran into you. Mind if I use your towel?"

"Yes, I do." Richard pointed toward a pile on a chair.

The man moved toward them with a quickness surprising in someone of his low-slung girth, and was back in seconds, wiping off the monk-fringe of his hair. "Aren't you going to introduce me?"

"No," Richard said.

The man held out his thick-fingered hand towards Karen. "George Edwards," he said.

She took his hand without enthusiasm, feeling Richard's resistance to the intrusion, at the same time noting the ring on the chubby man's finger, a replica of the one on Richard's. "Karen Sparks," she said politely.

"American," George noted, and pulled up a chair beside them. "Rich, I hope."

"I do wish you'd go away," said Richard.

"Is that any way to treat an old classmate?"

"You were in Richard's class?" Karen wondered aloud, George's appearance older than Richard's by a decade.

"Not literally. We were in the same year at Uppingham, but not all of us have the aristocratic heritage. So no matter how clever you are, you can never be in the same *class*."

"George, don't you have a buyout or a conglomerate to form somewhere?"

"Hong Kong, actually. This is a brief respite to get myself in shape."

"It isn't working," said Richard.

"Well, we can't all have athletic prowess and a family history of hair. Have you seen any of our other schoolmates?"

"Fortunately, no," Richard said.

"There's an amazing number of Uppingham alums in Asia," George said to Karen. "Surprisingly successful group."

"When do you leave for Hong Kong?" Richard asked impatiently.

"Probably not soon enough to suit you," said George.

"I could use a walk on the beach," Richard said, and reached for Karen, pulled her up from the chaise.

"Maybe we could have dinner or something later," George said. "They make a big thing here about barbecuing pigs. I'd be happy to host you."

"I don't like pork," said Richard, moving away.

"Then maybe we could just roast a black sheep," George called after them.

People flew kites on the beach in the gusty winds, a colorful distraction from the discussion initiated by George, which Karen understood Richard had no wish to continue, and so let drop in spite of her curiosity. Oversized kites, bird shaped, in outrageous colors, fuchsia, purple, royal blue, soared above the sands in front of the hotel, sitting on the air like hawks.

Richard invited Karen to lunch at a restaurant farther down the strand where the food, he said, was the best in Bali, and he'd be able to pick up the tab. "Even a rotter likes making the occasional gesture," he said as they walked along the shimmering foam at the ocean's edge, barefoot, sandals in hand.

"I think you enjoy calling yourself names," Karen said.

"You're the one who said I was dangerous."

"I'm not sure you really are."

"I could produce evidence, if you wanted. Or certainly George could, my fine fellow Uppinghamian."

"He's not very pleasant."

"Actually, George is quite funny, if you're not the butt of the joke."

"He's just jealous because you've kept your hair."

"You *are* generous. So quick to be on the side of people you think you like."

"I *know* I like you." She walked beside him and tried to ask her question casually, hoping it wouldn't sound like probing. "Is Lord Hensley your father?"

"Not anymore," Richard said.

A brown-skinned boy with glowing black eyes and an armful of kites approached them, a wide, white smile on his lean, lively face, revealing teeth that were smooth all the way across, no points on the incisors. A purple falcon kite rose and dipped above his head. "Mr. Richard . . ." he said, holding out the spool of string anchoring the kite.

"Not today, Wayan."

"Beautiful day. Beautiful sky. Beautiful wind. Beautiful lady . . ." He urged the spool toward them, grinning, guileless.

"How much are they?" Karen asked.

"Forty thousand rupiah," the boy said.

"She's with me, Wayan."

"Thirty thousand," said the boy. He saw the look on Richard's face. "Twenty."

"I'll have the purple one." Karen reached inside the small woven bag that hung from the string on her shoulder, gave him the money. Smiling his curiously even smile, he reinforced the wood slats in the frame of the kite, handed her the spool that held the string.

She started running with the kite. "Let it loose a little at a time," Wayan called after her.

She unrolled the spool as she ran. The wind carried the kite higher. Richard ran behind her, laughing. "You look like a little girl," he shouted.

To her surprise, she could feel her whole body blush. Maybe it was the heat of the day, but it felt as if it came from inside her rather than the sun, the warmth of being appreciated, acknowledged, admired. She ran faster down the beach, trailing the kite behind and above her, gusted as high by her feelings as the kite was by the wind. Richard made no attempt to keep pace with her, and so he couldn't, she hoped, catch how light-headed she was.

The restaurant served tasty pastas, crispy salads and not very good wines, seared tuna that had come that morning from the ocean. Set behind a grassy dune, the building was little more than a glorified hut with tables, two storied, thatch roofed, overlooking a row of palm trees and the sea.

They ate almost wordlessly, in spite of the many questions she had. It was a discipline she wasn't used to, keeping things inside, but she tried to adapt to his air of mystery, his being as unwilling to share his history as she was ready to spill her whole self on the table. The waiter looked at her interestedly as he laid the bill down and, passing her chair, picked up the purse she'd let slip to the floor. "Ma'am best be careful with this," the waiter said, handing it to her,

filling his few words with what seemed to be dispropor-
tionate caution.

"You see, everyone is looking out for you," Richard
said, sipping his wine, wiping his mouth with a linen napkin. "Everyone but me."

"I prefer your looking at me to looking *out* for me."

"You great, soft lump," he said, and squeezed her forearm. "Let me go settle up." He picked up the bill and went
inside to the office of the restaurant.

The Englishman they had seen at the pool came
bounding up the bamboo steps, curiously agile for his size
and build. "I'm sorry to intrude . . ." George started.

"Then don't," Karen interrupted, not really disliking
him as much as concerned at what she sensed he might be
going to say.

"But I feel it incumbent on me to give you fair warning. You seem a really nice woman," he said. "That's at
least a step up for Richard. Usually they're shallow,
empty . . ."

"I don't want to hear this," Karen said, though she did.

"Very well. But you ought at least to know you'll
doubtless have to carry the whole load. He ran through a
huge inheritance, and then embezzled his father's own
bank. Lord Hensley disowned him."

"You must be very envious of Richard," Karen said.

"Well, I admit life would have been easier with someone dropping a packet of money on me. But I wouldn't

have squandered it, or stolen, and I've done quite well just being hardworking and clever."

"And a gossip."

"I wouldn't have said anything if you hadn't seemed such a decent sort."

"Of course you would have," said Karen. "He probably did better than you at school."

"Only by shagging the teachers," George said.

"Please go away," she said, suffused with a new kind of heat, shock, disbelief, shame for a man she hardly knew but was terribly drawn to, chagrin for this round little carrier of tales, who, in spite of the bad news he seemed to be and bring, had something oddly likable about him.

"Well, George," Richard said, returning to the table, his face slightly ashen under the tan. "Still trying to get into clubs where they won't have you as a member?"

"I didn't realize there was anything exclusive about not wanting harm to come to people."

"We must not have seen each other for longer than I thought. I missed your whole transition from scandalmonger to benevolent soul."

"One must be given a good enough scandal to *mong*," said George. "May I offer you a pudding?"

"I wouldn't be able to swallow it," said Richard, pulling out Karen's chair, indicating she should follow him.

"Maybe you're afraid of just desserts."

Richard led her across a bridge over a stream near the restaurant, a marshy rivulet that widened and disappeared into the ocean. The bridge itself was made up of gray wooden slats, nailed together somewhat tenuously, with a weathered wooden handrail on either side. Richard held Karen's hand, leading her across it, backing toward the opposite bank, the bridge not really wide enough to accommodate the two of them side by side, and he, apparently, knowing it well enough not to have to watch where he was going. On the far side was a primitive parking lot, pebbles on soggy terrain, overlooking it an open Hindu temple, carved stone gods visible above the dark walls.

"Are we about to have a religious experience?" Karen asked, trailing her purple kite.

"I certainly hope so."

But instead of climbing the steps to the the temple, he led her past it, to a wide, thick wooden gate on the other side of the road. He pushed it open.

"*Et voilà . . .*" he said, ushering her inside a closed, grassy enclave, brilliant with wildflowers. To the left was a building little bigger than a teahouse, front porch with a railing of bamboo, two deeply cushioned chairs on thick bamboo bases like sentinels guarding the door. He took Karen's hand again and led her up the wooden steps. "This is where I live."

"Richard . . ."

"Let me teach you what you've forgotten," he said very softly, touching her. Birds twittered in the rice paddies adjacent, joyfully diving for food, undeterred by the handkerchiefs on sticks waving in the wind, the metallic clink of paddles, the Balinese equivalent of scarecrows, charmingly ineffective. "Let me remind you . . ." His fingers moved down her belly.

"I haven't . . ." she said, pulling away, flushed with the heat he aroused in her, little pinpricks of longing where he'd touched her, confusion about getting involved with a man about whom she knew nothing but the terrible things she'd just heard and didn't want to believe. "I haven't forgotten."

"Don't you want me?"

"Of course I do."

"Then what's wrong? What are you afraid of?" He pushed open the front door. "You see? No locks. Everything open. Including me."

"Then why won't you tell me what happened with your father?"

"Didn't George tell you? That fat little fop. Suddenly able to move with the speed of light, such was his hurry to make me look bad to you." He stared at her hard. "What exactly did he say?"

"Something about your inheritance. Your father's bank."

"Well, you might as well hear it all," Richard said, color draining from beneath his tan, his skin taking on the grayish tone it had when he'd said the word *disgrace*. "Lord Hensley despised me."

"Why do you refer to him as Lord Hensley?"

"He was always so distant. Demanding of respect. Hardly a man one would call 'Dad.' Even 'Father' seemed too warm. Very early in my life he gave up all pretense of caring, and outright loathed me."

"Why?"

"His mother left me everything. Money he assumed would be his. Was it my fault Granny loved me more? Took me for tea at Harrod's every Thursday when I was a little boy. Spoilt me dreadfully. Piles of whipped cream on my scones. Piles of toys on my birthday. Piles of money when she died." His eyes misted over, genuine, deep, as he seemed to become conscious of the loss, what it had felt like to be really loved. Then true feeling seemed erased from them, and glib mischief returned. "I spent it, of course. Ran through it all. Cars. Tailored clothes. Glamorous evenings at Anabel's. Stunning, empty, silly women I tried to spoil like Granny spoilt me. The last of them lost interest when the money ran out, and threatened to leave me.

"So I went to work at Father's bank. Naturally he was not about to give me much of a salary, so I borrowed a few thousand without the usual loan application. Had every intention of returning it. But an auditor found the discrepancy before I had a chance.

"Lord Hensley gave me just enough money to get out of England and avoid a scandal, with strict instructions never to return."

"Maybe he didn't mean it."

"Of course he did. I'd committed the unpardonable sin."

"Embezzlement?"

"The theft of love. Making his mother love me more than she did her own son. Of course there's no danger of that happening with you and Seth." He put his arm around her.

"Are you ever homesick for England?"

"This is where I was meant to be. For all my endless days."

There was no mistaking the wistfulness of his tone. His wounded spirit, like his wounded mouth, moved her. She wanted to reach for the hurt, touch it, heal it.

From where they stood on his porch, they could see saffron-robed monks on the beach floating flowers into the sea. The monks threw protesting ducks into the water, pushed them underneath as they quacked to the surface. "What are they doing?" Karen asked.

"It's a ceremony. Blessing a baby, or sending someone's ashes into the afterlife, probably. Making an offering to the gods."

"Can't you make it up with them?"

"The gods or the ducks?"

"Your family."

"They don't want to know if I'm alive or dead."

"That can't be true."

"But it is," he said, and the sorrow in his tone said it was.

He pushed open his door. It was completely ajar now, and she could see inside. The house seemed to consist of only one room, not very wide, just a few feet longer than the single, metal-framed bed against the right wall. The bed was covered with a batik spread, swirls of black and white, a whiter white than the paint on the walls, cracked and, in places, peeling. At the far end of the room was another open door, leading to a bathroom just a notch above squalor. She felt a rush of pity for him, banished from the Eden that was the British upper class, to the Eden that was Bali, where it still helped to have money.

He took her arm, just above the elbow, and urged her gently inside. "So now you know my sorry tale."

"If it's true."

"Why would I confess such terrible things about myself if they were lies?"

"To cover yourself in case I'd heard them from George."

"George couldn't have known about Granny and my . . ."—he seemed hardly able to say the word—". . . father," he managed. "Why would I tell you that?"

"To touch my heart."

"And have I?" He put his hand to her breast, lightly traced the contours of it through the sarong she had wound around her bathing suit, his crystal blue eyes fixed on the fabric as he did so, the expression in them unabashedly sensual. "Can I?" There was an unexpected subtlety in his fingers, like feathers, grazing, lifting, fine.

He raised his eyes to hers, let his hands trail slowly up over her chest to her throat, brought them to rest beneath her chin and lifted it, so that she had to look at him squarely. Then he put his mouth on hers. Gently this time. Barely touching. Teasing. Tasting. A butterfly's kiss. But in counterpoint to the gentleness, he pressed himself against her, hard.

She took his hands from her face and backed away. "Why were you with those women if they were silly and empty?"

"I suppose I was silly and empty myself."

"And I'm supposed to think you've changed?"

"You're not supposed to think," he said, and kissed her again. She did not respond. "We have less than two weeks," he said.

She turned her back to him.

"It's this place, isn't it? It's so shabby."

"The place is fine."

"Look, I could have lied about the women and said they were wonderful. But I haven't been exposed to that many wonderful women before you."

His words moved her, as they were doubtless meant to. But she still wasn't sure. "I'm not used to the heat." She tried to make the pronouncement light with double meaning, even while she wondered how he slept at night, with the weight of the humidity on his skin.

"I should put the air-con on," he said.

"Why don't you?"

"I don't have any," he said miserably, suddenly pale beneath the deep tan again, as though feelings of inadequacy robbed him of blood. "You should be with someone who could cover you with comfort, treat you like the queen you are."

"I'm not a queen."

"You could have fooled me," he said.

"Then I'm learning," she said, lightly. "I've never known how to fool anybody."

He grabbed her from behind, put his hands roughly on her breasts, pulled her toward him so there was no separation, thrust himself against her buttocks. The harshness of the gesture saved her as much as her own ambivalence.

"Don't do that," she said angrily, as disappointed with the coarse action as she'd been with his kiss. It was gentleness she wanted, tenderness, more than sex. There was a saying she'd heard that men tolerated affection because they wanted sex, and women put up with sex because they wanted affection. It seemed less a homily now than a painful truth, since she'd been robbed of both, and knew how deeply she'd been stirred by a kiss, even a bad one.

"You don't really want me," he said, petulantly.

"Not like that," she said.

"I shall give up on you then," he said, and skittered down to the sand without looking back at her.

"Not yet," she wanted to shout at him. "Woo me. Court me. Change my mind with sweet words, move me with gentle kisses." But instead, all she did was run, and fall into step beside him.

Four

TELL ME what happened to your mouth," she said, cajoling, as they walked barefoot on the wet sand.

"I've already told you far too much," he said. "You bloody forthright Americans. You understand nothing of the value of secrecy."

"Secrecy or duplicity?"

"I am *not* duplicitous," he said angrily. "What I *don't* tell you can never be a lie."

"That's about as duplicitous as you can get."

"Is it?" he said, fierce now. "I thought it was pretty direct. Maybe you ought to just run, and keep running. Maybe you ought to find George. He'll certainly tell you just what's on his mind, small as it is."

"I don't want George," she said.

"What do you want?"

"You," she kept herself from saying. "I want to know what happened to your mouth," she spoke aloud.

He looked at her sideways, checking her out, and started to speak, somewhat grudgingly. "Well, first there was rugby," he said. "A number of smashes to the face with a well-kicked ball. Wired jaw. That sort of thing." The recollection of how well he'd gotten over what he'd been through seemed to catch his fancy, as the words became melodic, a song of his own prankishness he sang to himself. "Then there was drink, during my flush time. Falling fashionably down the stairs at Anabel's after losing thousands. Then there were drugs, while I wandered through Asia, wondering where to go, not particularly mindful of where I was. Capital offense in Singapore, you know, carrying drugs. Fortunately I got swacked out of my head the last time in Kuala Lumpur, and woke up in a pool of blood. They flew me to Singapore for the repair with nothing in my pockets but a passport. Some banker friend of Lord Hensley's staked me to plastic surgery and passage here."

"I thought your father wrote everybody not to lend you money."

"Not to go into business, or so it would help me lift my head, regain my vanquished pride. But most of them have sons, and I suppose my mouth would have been a blemish on all British youth."

"It's a marvelous mouth," she could not help but say, the flush of her own attraction deepened by what he had finally told her so seemingly glibly, that was, she was sure, underscored with pain.

"Easy to say now that we're back out in public, where I can't ravish you. Maybe we can go to your room, with the air-con on."

"Seth is probably back by now."

"My nemesis."

"He doesn't mean to be. He could use a friend." She stopped on the sand, looked at him. "So could I."

"You mean, rather than a lover?" He looked a little peaked again beneath his tan, as he did when he spoke of his disgrace, the common place he lived, his father, all the failures in his life. It was as though the self-assurance that smacked of arrogance had weakness behind it, a vampire shadow, draining him, showing itself when he was fearful about what he really was. Or wasn't.

"I'd like to have both."

"Then you shall," he said.

Seth was in the bathtub when she got back to their room. The afternoon sunlight coming through the atrium was deflected by lush foliage, but even with the glare softened, Karen could see how burned he was. His face, ears, neck, arms and legs were a scarlet she could feel without touching.

"Oh, sweetheart," she said. "Why didn't you use sun-block?"

"I did," he said. "It was no match for Bali. Like Woody Allen fighting George Foreman."

"Do you hurt?"

"Do you breathe?" he said.

"I should never have let you go out on your own. I knew something awful would happen."

"It's only a sunburn," he said. "I'll live."

"I'll get some salve from the drug store."

"I already did." His eyes looked gold against the red of his skin, the leonine hair almost platinum. The assertive arc of his nose, the bold, manly curve of it, seemed diminished by the clusters of freckles now sprouted all over the bridge, a sign of the defenseless boy he really was. "I charged it. I hope that's all right."

"Of course it is."

"You may not recognize my writing. I could hardly move my hand."

"Oh, Seth, I'm so sorry."

"For what?" he said, moving a washcloth across his stomach. "It's my own fault. Not like I needed a mother to protect me. Anyway, you weren't here." He looked away. "Where were you?"

"I had lunch at a restaurant down the beach."

"It must have been a very long lunch."

"It's a really good restaurant. We'll have to go there together."

"The three of us?"

"You and me."

"Is that grammatically correct? Isn't it you and I, or is it you and the wastrel?"

"Stop it."

"You didn't get much color. I guess you were inside."

"It has a thatched roof."

"His place?"

"The restaurant."

"But you *were* with him?"

"You could have come with us."

"I had a date with Destiny. It was my time to learn about not getting burned." He looked at her directly. "I hope you know about that one."

There was a cocktail party on the terrace outside the lobby for the guests that evening, an attempt at the formality the hotel didn't have but probably imagined a European clientele wanted. Although the majority of the guests were Australians, all Caucasians were referred to as "Europeans," to distinguish them from Asians, and, most particularly, the Japanese. In spite of the financial turmoil in Japan, its populace seemed still to be traveling everywhere, and in large groups. The luxury hotels gave out no particular instructions to staff or suggestions in their manuals, but the unspoken truth was that there *was* a quota, an actual percentage of

Japanese the better hotels did not wish to go over, as they eagerly courted Westerners.

Reluctantly, Seth put on long pants and a T-shirt with a designer decal on it, which he had pronounced "wussy," a new word in his vocabulary that Karen hadn't heard before. He made some plaintive, aching sounds as he slipped it over his head, and she winced for him.

But once out on the terrace, with a tropical fruit punch in his hand, he became actually sociable. He was talking to a Welsh ecologist who'd just made a speaking tour of Australia. Seth was chatting affably, chest puffed out in a manner reminiscent of his father, the big, amiable man who'd made everybody feel at home, even when it was in their own houses.

"Hey, Mom," he signaled her over. "Come say hello to Peter Andrews. Peter Andrews, this is my mother. Karen Sparks."

"A pleasure," the Englishman said. He was white haired, in his sixties.

"Mr. Andrews is saving the planet."

"Not quite. I'm lecturing on the greenhouse effect. Hoping people will listen in time."

"You see, not everybody is just looking out for themselves," Seth said pointedly.

"Unfortunately, most people are," said the Englishman. "Throughout Asia, of course, it's not a conscious choice. They can't worry about what's down the road when what matters is rice in the bowl today. Is this your first time in Bali?"

"We just got here yesterday," Karen said, her attention wandering, her eyes on the lit portion of the beach.

"You must be sure to see Kitamani. It's a deep crater that houses an active volcano."

"My mom is really good about finding those."

"Excuse me," said Karen, and pulling her son aside, spoke to him in muted tones. "No more digs about Richard. You're not being very subtle."

"Well, why are you being so cold to Mr. Andrews? He's the kind of guy you should be meeting. Distinguished. Older."

"I don't need you to play matchmaker."

"Sure you do."

"There's a pretty girl over there. She looks about your age. Why don't you go talk to her?"

"I'm not interested in anyone who makes sense," said Seth. "I'm going to get involved with some Mata Hari who'll chew me up and spit me out and take me for everything I'm worth."

"Why are you giving me such a hard time?"

"Because I love you. Because if I give you a hard time maybe someone else won't give you a hard time who would really give you a hard time."

"I appreciate your concern," she said. "But I can take care of myself."

"I know you can," Seth said. "But I don't know if you

really know that. You're a very strong woman, Mom. You did great with Dad. How you took care of him. A lot of people would have fallen apart going through that illness with someone they loved, but you didn't. Don't do it now."

She saw Richard come onto the lit sands beyond the dunes, and her whole face brightened. Seth followed her gaze.

"Oh, shit," he said.

"Watch your mouth *and* your manners," she said.

"You watch them," he grumbled, heading for the path to their room. "I'm going to bed."

Candles in hurricane lamps on the tables, flowers at each setting, gave an extra fillip of romance to the open-air restaurant Richard had taken her to, a touch the place didn't really need. Everything about Bali seemed gorgeously excessive, like the heat, like the moisture in the air, like the sensuality that came even with the wind. Richard was being gentle now, subtle, as though he'd started to understand what she was feeling, tracing the skin on the back of her hand. Making a kind of love to it, his finger moving slowly around and in between each one of hers.

She flinched a little as he touched the corner of her hand, where carelessly she'd neglected to spread sunblock. "You're burned," he said, concern on his face.

"It's just a tiny place," she said. "I didn't realize how strong the sun was even when you make an effort to stay out of it."

"We'll attend to that later," he said soothingly, and signaled for the waitress.

He'd been apologetic about bringing her to this particular restaurant, even as he said it was the best place to eat, because he couldn't afford to take the check. But that didn't bother her. What bothered her was Seth not being with them. Because Seth was absent, she was not quite there with Richard. Her attention wandered as it had on the terrace while the ecologist spoke to her, when what she was doing was waiting for her would-have-been lover. Now that Richard was present, she could feel the absence of her son.

"You're someplace else," Richard said, studying her face. "It's a bit early in our relationship for you to be bored."

"I'm not in the least bored," she said.

His complexion looked somehow ruddier than it had that afternoon. "But you don't seem happy."

"Of course I am."

"Do you always look unhappy when you're happy?"

She smiled. She could sense her own discomfort, the forced nature of the smile.

"If you'll excuse me for a moment," he said, getting up from his bamboo chair, wiping his mouth with a napkin although they had not yet eaten. "I'm going to call in the Fusiliers."

"What are you going to do?"

"Why, I shall lift Seth from his slough of despond, and bring him here bodily if I have to. Get him to join us."

"He's hurting from his sunburn," she said. "If I can feel what I feel on this little corner of my hand, he must be really uncomfortable. We should leave him alone."

"I would leave him alone if he really were alone, but he's got you with him. I want you here with me." He left the restaurant.

"I thought you were my sandwich," Seth said, opening the door.

"You want to eat in your room on a night like this?" Richard said, pointing to the stars, a canopy of light. "So many of the people in the world can't even see the stars, the lights of their cities are so bright. There are more stars here than are dreamt of in your philosophy."

"That isn't how the quote goes," Seth said.

"But you do have a philosophy?"

"I guess."

"You want to tell me what it is?"

Seth looked at the Englishman carefully. "It's about not hurting people. It's about how you don't take advantage of someone who's . . . What's the word when someone has no defenses?"

"Vulnerable?" Richard said.

"Yeah, that's right. Vulnerable. Not kicking someone when they're down."

"Well, that's not exactly a philosophy," Richard said. "That's a credo. And a good one, I grant you. But if you're interested in philosophy, you might want to read this." He reached into his fanny pack, and took out a well-worn copy of Walt Whitman's *Leaves of Grass*.

"Yucch," Seth said. "Isn't this the book of poems Bill gave Monica? *And* Hillary?"

"That doesn't diminish its value," Richard said.

"It does for me," Seth said, but took the book anyway. "You expect me to read it right now?"

"No, as a matter of fact, I was hoping you'd join us for dinner."

"I'm not hungry."

"Then why did you order a sandwich?"

"I'm tired of fruit."

"Come on," Richard said. "Give us *both* a break. You *and* me. You might even have fun. Your behaving like this is making me look good by comparison. Certainly you don't want to do that."

"You're right. I'll get dressed."

"Good boy," said Richard, and clapped him on the shoulder.

Seth flinched. "Owww."

"Sorry," Richard said. "I've got some herbs for that. I'll make a poultice for you after dinner."

"I think I'll have . . ." Seth addressed the waitress. The sound of bells and primitive pipes filled the restaurant, a Balinese orchestra of men and women playing the gamelan, an elaborately painted and gilded wood and brass instrument, like a three-tiered xylophone. They wore costumes as ornate as the instrument, costumes fretted with gold. ". . . the broiled poultice."

"Pardon?" said the waitress.

Seth turned to Richard, who sat across the table, on Karen's right. "What exactly is a poultice?"

"A wet compress."

"I thought it was a fish," Seth said, and turned toward the waitress. "I'll have the grilled shrimp."

She left with their order.

Sweetcakes and palm leaves curled into fantasy shapes sat at the base of the gamelan. Seth strained his head to look. "They going to feed that thing?" he asked.

"Everything in Bali is believed to have powers—a musical instrument has a spirit that has to be kept alive with offerings," Richard said. "They're asking the spirit of the gamelan for beauty."

Karen's attention was pulled toward the music, the sound of it, the curious rhythms. It was literally foreign to what she was used to hearing and the kind of songs she had written, but still it magnetized her, magical. She had never sung to Richard, or talked much about her music. There seemed to be too much weight on her side of the scale already, without adding to it the fact that she was accomplished, that her songs had been more than a little popular, when his own history was so empty of success.

"Paying homage"—he pronounced it "home-age"—"to a musical instrument," Seth remarked. "Why don't they just get a synthesizer? They could beat the shit out of it, and it wouldn't care."

"Language," Karen said.

"I don't mean to challenge you," said Richard. "But he is rather colorful."

"It's my skin," Seth said.

Richard smiled. "I'm glad you decided to join us."

"Me, too." Seth looked intensely at Richard. "So you're also a medicine man?"

"I make no claim to that."

"Then what's with the herbs?"

"When you live someplace like Bali, with so many priests and healers, where the whole base of the culture is spiritual, you can't help learning things." Richard reached for a piece of bread, broke off a little. "Unless, of course, you're incredibly stubborn and fixed in your thinking."

"You talking about me?" Seth's eyes narrowed.

"I'm talking about myself, the way I was when I first came. Convinced I was smarter than anyone, certainly smarter than the simple people who live here. But often we confuse education with wisdom."

"You've gotten wise?"

"I'm working on it. You should really try the Gado Gado. It's a lightly cooked salad of sprouts, tofu, all the vegetables of Bali, very crunchy, with a spicy peanut sauce. So tasty it's hard to believe it's good for you, but it's loaded with vitamins." He pronounced it with a short *i*.

"A dietician, too," Seth said.

"It was just a suggestion."

"I'd like to try that," Karen said.

Richard signaled the waitress to come back and ordered it for Karen. "Also we'd like a large bottle of vinegar. Cider vinegar if you have it."

"You don't wish the normal dressing?" the waitress asked.

"This is to take with us," Richard said, and smiled at Seth. "That's how we'll take the sting out of your sunburn. Vinegar and lavender. We'll have you pain-free in no time."

"So you are the Wizard, after all," Seth said.

Karen watched their interaction in silence, like an observer in a tennis match, wishing that the two would enjoy playing with each other, and so make easier whatever future relationship there was to be. Not that she imagined for a moment Richard could be as important in her life as her son. The most this could be, she knew in her rational mind, was a fling.

But just thinking that pulled at something in her, it went so against her grain. She had always made love because *love* was what it was. There had been no casual *amours* in her history. With the few men who'd proceeded Charley, she'd convinced herself she loved them, hoped that they would love her. Already old-fashioned when her day was dawning, she knew her attitude would seem antique now. Still, she could not envision entering into a quick, unemotional coupling, no matter how great her physical desires. To care for someone without becoming attached was not part of her emotional makeup. She was terrible at letting go.

Here she was, the affair not even begun, already worried about how she would be able to deal with its ending. Flashing in the back of her mind were the decorator sheets she'd liked in the linen department of her favorite department store, grieving on a minor scale over having no one to buy them for. Making what was not yet even a defined moment into a long-term future. Not even holding yet, and already holding on.

Once in her life, only once, had she let go with grace. But she'd had no choice, really. By trying to hold on, she only would have made it harder for Charley.

After dinner, in the hotel room, Richard made poultices of lavender soaked in vinegar inside soft towels, and put them on Seth's bright red places. First he lay him on his stomach, and soothed the backs of his legs and neck. Then he had Seth turn over, and did the same to the scarlet places on the front, including his cheeks. During that phase, Seth studied Richard's face, while Karen, sitting on the other bed, tried to seem not to supervise what was going on between them. She noted Seth's skepticism, watched it recede gradually into relief.

"May I have your hand?" Richard asked Karen.

"Are you proposing to her?" Seth said, barely concealing his alarm.

"She has a small burn on the back of it," Richard said. He took her hand across his knee, soothed the scarlet corner with a tiny poultice.

"That stuff really works," Seth said with surprise.

"I'm glad." Richard smiled at him, put Karen's hand back on her own lap, the poultice still on it.

"Why are your teeth so even?" Seth asked. "Everybody here has these big, wide white smiles, and all their teeth are even. It's unnatural."

"Quite right," Richard said, dipping a large poultice back into the bowl of vinegar on the floor, squeezing, and, handing the towel to Karen, indicated she should put it on Seth. She got up from the bed and applied it gingerly, afraid really to touch her son, fearful of intensifying discomfort she guiltily felt she had caused, letting him go off on his own into the punishing sunlight.

"There's a ceremony," Richard explained to Seth. "It's

supposed to come at puberty. Tooth filing. The priest grinds the canines down so there are no points, and that's supposed to tame your animal nature. Get rid of the beast, as it were. Lose aggression and anger."

"Does it work?"

"Difficult for a Westerner to even understand. But that's why the Balinese are so good-natured and pleasant."

"Because of their teeth?" Seth asked.

"Because they don't want to be angry. Anger serves no purpose. Only hurts the one who feels it."

"Depends how hard you hit," said Seth.

"They send a man to jail for fighting here."

"No kidding," Seth said. "So you wanted to be like that? Without anger?"

"I don't remember. I did it when I was drunk."

"Like a sailor with a tattoo," Seth said. "Only now you can't get your pointy teeth back."

"I don't want them. I like not getting mad."

"It really works?"

"Seems to."

"I'd hate not to be able to get mad," Seth said. "There's so much bullshit in the world."

"Language," Karen said.

"No other word for it, Mom. Right?" he asked Richard.

"I'm afraid that really does say it."

Seth smiled. "I'm glad you got drunk. I'd hate to think

you were trying to pass yourself off as perfect. That would make me really mad."

"So do you like him better than you did?" Karen asked Seth, when Richard had gone home for the night. There'd been time for only a light kiss outside the door, with Seth waiting inside.

"I wouldn't go that far," Seth said. "I don't *not* like him as much as I didn't before."

"I'll settle for that."

"Maybe what you should do," Seth said, rolling over on his side, wincing a little as he did so, facing her, "is learn that you don't have to settle. You're entitled to the best."

"Thank you for thinking that."

"He isn't the best. He doesn't even come close."

"I don't want to discuss it. He was really kind to you. Why can't you accept that?"

"But I can. I can accept that he was kind. It would be nice to be able to think he didn't do it just to make a better impression."

"On whom?"

"On meem. He doesn't need to do anything more to fascinate you," Seth said. "You've been sandbagged." He got up from the cot and headed for the bathroom. "I think I'll go in and brush my points."

Karen lay back on the bed, looking at the fan whirring

slowly on the ceiling. She mused on Richard's unexpected, welcome tenderness toward both of them, and fixed her mind on the place on her hand where the pain had been eased. She wondered where the poultice was that could do that with life.

Sleeping, Seth was the child again, the same little boy she had doted on when he was four. Sleep soothed his features back into cherub.

She had awakened early. It was still dark when she'd gotten out of bed, gone out into her little courtyard, and lain on a chaise, looking at the heavens till the stars disappeared into the day.

Part of her reverie was a nostalgic one. She thought about Charley, and how much he would have enjoyed this place. Then she revised sentimentality with realism, and knew he would have bristled at the length of the trip, hated the heat, the humidity. So she'd let herself slip into erotic musing, touched the skin of her inner arm as Richard had, checked it for softness, resiliency. It felt moist, silky to her own fingers, like a girl's. Had it seemed so to him? She felt giddy, aroused more by memory than she'd been by the actuality, the soft brush of his hair against her cheeks silkier in fantasy.

She was glad that they hadn't made love. She wasn't sure yet about him, for all he had told her of his supposed history. He had highlighted his penchant for dishonesty. Even his finally seeming to open up to her a little might have been a lie. She had no way of affirming if it was safe to trust. She knew herself too well—there was no way she could let a man inside her without his becoming part of her.

But in spite of her wish for caution, she longed for him. In the early morning hours, not so much fresh from sleep as ripened by it, she felt languorous. She was sorry now he was not there to touch her in the darkness. The sky was filled with glints of approaching light, sparking excited feelings in her body, like remembrance of his hands on her, remembrance of how rich it was to feel fully alive. So what did she imagine she was waiting for?

Restless, Karen had come back inside, sat on the couch by the cot, and watched Seth sleeping, as she'd done when he was an infant, content simply to watch him, unable to believe she had such a whole, healthy son. Taking pleasure from seeing he really existed, listening to him breathe.

He felt her looking at him now, and opened his eyes. "I dreamed about Richard," Seth said. "He was taking classes in how to seem sincere."

"Why do you wake up with negative words?"

"Why is that negative? He was doing really well. He almost convinced *me*." He got out of bed and went toward the bathroom, and just before shutting the door, turned to Karen and said, "There are more things in heaven and earth than are dreamed of in *Leaves of Grass*."

Just before they left for breakfast, Karen took her minia-ture keyboard out of the drawer and set it on top of the dresser, as if being exposed to the air of Bali might be good for it, as it was for her. Little shafts of melody were starting to form in her brain, the first glimmers of music since Charley died, but she had not yet made an attempt to write anything, frightened that song wouldn't be there.

She and Seth were silent on the way to breakfast. A hotel worker gathered fallen frangipani blossoms from the paths. A gardener trimmed hibiscus bushes, interrupting his labor with a beaming, brilliantly white, even-toothed smile. *"Salamat Pagi."*

"Salamat Pagi," Seth said happily in return. He had already mastered most of the little book of Balinese phrases Karen had bought him. He knew the salutes for the differ-ent times of day, that *pagi* was morning. The greeting changed every few hours, at midday becoming "Good Af-ternoon," in late day "Good Twilight," "Good Evening" in the darkness, "Good Night," and finally "Good Dreams": *"Salamat Mimpi."* As though every interval in the life of a human were a separate block of time, to be celebrated.

Maybe it was. Maybe she had been foolish to let even moments of her life go by uncommemorated. Maybe it was not too late to learn to make it all a celebration.

On a sun-washed terrace, protected by oversized umbrellas, she and Seth sat down to breakfast. A waiter
brought them menus, and that morning's *International
Herald-Tribune*. Karen was glad to have it to hide behind,
absorbing herself in the as-nearly-always-disturbing head-
lines, bad news on a global level somehow being a sanctuary from personal confusion.

Her son studied her as he drank his juice. Then he
wiped his mouth meticulously with his napkin, as he'd seen
Richard do, twice around the upper lip and mustache area,
checking the corners, blotting the lower lip three times. It
was as if something might hang there besides food. Old
mistakes. Words that had been better unspoken. Somehow
the gesture imitated made the original seem a tic, a nervous
habit rather than impeccable table manners.

"Do you want to try the potato with scrambled eggs
and caviar?" Karen asked him.

"Yucch."

"Every once in a while I forget you're an adolescent.
And then you hit me with one of those sounds."

"My adolescence is over. I am a full-grown man, or my
voice would still be cracking, and the bones in my knees
wouldn't have knitted."

"Then why do you use those awful expressions? A simple 'No, thank you,' would do."

"A simple no, thank you," he said, and then, to the
waiter, "I'll have the cold cereal."

The beach had lost its metallic early-morning shimmer.

Undulating rays of reflected heat from the sands hung just above the shoreline. Already there were peddlers proffering cases of knockoff Cartier, Rolex, Piaget watches, strings of conches, mother-of-pearl spoons, semirespectful of the boundaries they were not supposed to trespass, waiting on the sand, ready to pounce on potential patrons.

Seth studied his mother's face until she put the paper down. "What do you think of when you think of Dad?" he asked her.

"Loss."

"I don't mean your feelings," he said. "Although I don't mean to ignore your feelings. I mean, what does the thought of him bring to your mind, you know, as a person? What he *was*."

"Funny. Kind. Big. Sharp. Sweet. A protector."

"You think this guy could even stand in his *shadow*?"

"Your dad doesn't cast a shadow anymore," said Karen.

Five

IN THE QUIET of the late morning, Seth sat at the edge of the beach, shaded by the palms, reading the book of poems Richard had given him, headphones on his ears, his stereo set out on the sand. The young girl who had been at the cocktail party the night before shimmied by in her underfilled bikini. When she failed to catch his eye, she spoke aloud.

"Hi." She was about fifteen, her dark hair pulled back into a ponytail, caught with gold-threaded elastic. He did not hear her, so she lifted one of his headphones, pulling it away from his ear. "Hi," she said, again.

"Hello," he said disinterestedly, but half-set the one headphone back of his ear so that he could hear her and the music at the same time.

She smiled. She wore very heavy braces. "Where are you from?"

"New York," he said. "You?"

"Sydney," she said.

"How come you didn't say 'G'day?' We see all these ads for Australia, and they're always throwing another shrimp on the barby, and saying 'G'day.' "

"I knew you were an American. So I said 'Hi.' That looks like it's from the States." She pointed to the portable stereo equipment.

"State of the art," Seth said. "My mother's a songwriter."

The girl was shifting her weight from leg to leg, obviously waiting for an invitation to sit down. He didn't offer one. "Would you like to have lunch?" she asked, finally. "We could throw another shrimp on the barby."

"I'm sorry. I'm off shrimp. I think of them as sea cockroaches."

She made a face. It went with her braces. "I believe you've made me go off them as well. Do you always have that effect on people?"

"Whenever I can," Seth said, and went back to his book.

She stood there for a moment, obviously hoping. But his eyes were fixed on the page. Letting out a little sigh, giving a shrug to her bony shoulders, she went up the grassy dune toward the pool.

"You certainly didn't seem very cordial to her," Richard said, coming up from the beach, surfboard under his naked arm, a tank top over his bathing suit. "Why were you so unfriendly?"

"She has no tits." Seth took the headphones off.

"I can understand that," Richard said. "Breasts are a fine attribute of women."

"My mother's in the room," Seth said.

"I'm looking for you."

"Why?"

"I'm going to teach you how to surf."

"I don't want to learn."

"How could you not?" Richard asked, and setting the board on the grassy dune, sat down on it. "It's great fun. And your mother said you ski."

"I like skiing. I should be away skiing right now."

"You're only good at the one sport?"

"I'm good at *all* sports," Seth said.

"So am I. That's how I earn my living."

Seth put down the book, and looked at Richard skeptically. "You earn a living?"

"The best I can. I teach surfing, all kinds of water sports, take tourists on hikes, white-water rafting."

"Really?" Seth said interestedly.

"Well, the last I haven't done for a while," Richard said, a shadow moving across his face.

"And you can make a living doing that?"

"Quite a good one," Richard said, sitting up straight. "Especially by Bali standards."

"You wouldn't rather be in the United States, living in luxury?"

"But I do live in luxury," Richard said, and lay on his back on the grass, looking at the sky. "A day like this is a luxury. Any day one wakes without pain and can see colors is a luxury. Look. All the different greens. The vibrant yellow of the flowers. The blue of the sky."

"You made your point," Seth said, interrupting. "I suppose there are a lot of people who would consider your life enviable."

"But not you?"

"Not me because I can see what you're *really* after."

"And that is?"

"I don't have to tell you. We both know."

"Why don't you get the chip off your shoulder and let me help you enjoy your vacation?"

"I'm not really on vacation," Seth said confidentially. "I'm on a mission."

"Really? What?"

"It's kind of a secret mission. But I guess I can share it with you, since you're part of it."

"I am?"

"Totally. I'm here to see my mother doesn't get hurt."

"What makes you think I'd hurt her?"

"You're a hurting kind of guy. An e'er-do-well."

"It's ne'er-do-well."

"Well, you know what I mean. And you know I'm right. She deserves better."

"I thoroughly agree. But for some reason she seems to have taken a fancy to me. I can't imagine you'd want to make her unhappy."

"*I* wouldn't be the one to make her unhappy."

Richard lay back on the dune, his hands behind his head. "How are you enjoying *Leaves of Grass*?"

"It's a little wussy."

"I'm not familiar with that word."

"It's a cross between wimp and pussy. No guts. No real balls."

"But Whitman had plenty of them: to say how he felt, to see as he saw, to show what he was."

"Gay?"

"I don't think that has anything to do with the power of the poetry—his or anyone else's. Even Shakespeare. His love sonnets might in fact have been written to Christopher Marlowe."

"It would never have worked as a movie," Seth said.

"It must be tiring to be so much wiser than your years," Richard said, a half smile on his face.

"It is lonely sometimes," he said ingenuously.

"You might have been nicer to that girl."

"Have you ever kissed someone with braces?"

"Well, as a matter of fact, I had my jaw broken a time or two playing rugby, and they had to wire it shut. I tried to kiss like that, and all I could use was the very edge of my mouth. It hurt like blazes."

"Imagine being on the receiving end."

"You're a very compassionate fellow," said Richard. "Thinking how someone else would feel."

"I was thinking of myself," said Seth.

"Were you?" He sat up and looked at Seth squarely, held his gaze, waited for a moment. "Aren't you still? Aren't you always?"

"I don't need you to teach me what's right," Seth said fiercely, and getting up from the chaise, dropped the book at Richard's bare feet and started up towards the villa. "You *or* your gay friends."

"I've made tremendous inroads with your son," Richard said. He and Karen were the only patrons in the bar, a pavilion, airy, the shape of an Indonesian *bale,* shady and thatch roofed, open to the breeze that blew through it gently but effectively, cooling them as their drinks were doing. The beverages were in tall, slender glasses, colorful fruit punches, well iced, with tiny paper umbrellas sticking up from the straws. "He doesn't dislike me anymore."

"Really?" The liveliness of her eyes was shaded by her growing infatuation, so her lids hung a little heavy, as though she were slightly drunk. There was no arguing he was handsome and charming. That he'd gone to the trouble of caring for her son, in the physical sense at least, was reassuring. All in all she had been measuring what there was to lose, and it added up to nothing but time. Another chance, when she'd thought her chance was over. She could feel herself melting, even without the moist heat around her.

A pale green sarong with gold threads was knotted just above her breasts, beneath it a bathing suit. The little sun she had exposed herself to had altered the color of her skin, turning it a golden bronze, shades lighter than Richard's tan but warm, healthy looking. Her face was darker as well, intensifying the brown of her eyes, making them seem almost black, deepened by what she was allowing herself to feel when she looked at him. It speeded up her heartbeat.

"Doesn't dislike me," Richard said. *"Loathes* me."

"But that isn't like Seth," she said unhappily. "He's a very tolerant boy."

"Not when he feels threatened."

"You really think you threaten him?"

"Oh, my sweet," he said, and ran his fingers around the outside curve of her ear. "He can't imagine it will end when you leave here."

"Do you?"

"I know it will."

"Then it's just as well we don't start it."

"But it's already in motion. Unstoppable."

She moved a little away. He looked at her, surprised.

"You couldn't possibly have thought this could go anywhere?"

"Of course not," she said, swallowing. "Not possibly."

"Though it would be lovely to be with you in the cool.

To stroke you, and taste you, and ease my way inside you in some temperate clime." He blew on her neck.

She trembled.

"It's times like this when I really hate what I am."

"What?"

"Poor," he said. "I should like to make love to you in a palace. I have a friend who has palaces, a genuine Balinese prince, but his palaces are open like this is. Bali style."

"I like Bali style."

"But not to make love in, in the heat of noon. You should have Bali style, but with Air-Con." His delivery capitalized the word. "That shall become my greatest ambition. To comfort you, and make love to you, and whisper words of passion to you. . . ."

"Your greatest ambition?"

"While you're here."

"And when I'm gone?"

"Why then, I shall have no ambition at all. I shall be the beachcomber your son thinks I am."

"No ambition at all?"

"None," he said. "Why should I have?"

"People feel better about themselves if they want to be something."

"Do they?" He looked at her, head tilted slightly so that his eyes angled mischief, bright blue, teasing. "They'd rather be some*thing* than some*one*? Was it more important to you being a songwriter than a person?"

"The joy came from both."

"When are you going to let me hear your songs?"

"When are you going to try and build a real life for yourself?"

"You see? You're already trying to change me. And that could be fatal. It might mean you're falling in love."

"Would that be so bad?"

"The worst thing that could happen."

"Why?"

"Because this is only for *here*." He curled her hair. "You musn't grow attached to me."

"And what if I'm the kind of person who can't take an affair lightly?"

"It's never too late to learn."

"Not even in my case?"

"Especially not in your case. You're a clever woman. And I'm a good teacher." He leaned to kiss her. It was a kiss transformed from his earliest kiss, transformed by her demonstration to him, serving now to transform her.

"You've been practicing," she said.

"Well, I'm as good a pupil as I am a teacher," he said proudly. "Let's go somewhere we can practice on each other."

He took her once again to the restaurant on the beach, the one he could afford. They had drinks with their lunch. She was unused to drinking in the daytime. She knew she

was giving herself a reverse safety net, an excuse to slide. A
young excuse, a sophomoric excuse. But that's what she
was again, sophomoric. A wise fool. More fool, she suspected, than wise.

But she didn't care anymore. She was ready for him, as
she had been ready for little else in her life, so revved up in
her imagination, so fired up inside her flesh that the air
seemed actually cool to her in comparison to what she was
experiencing. She could hardly touch her food.

Richard saw she wasn't eating. He signaled for the
check, paid it quickly. He took her by the hand, led her
toward the narrow wooden bridge over the stream. As they
crossed, he stopped for a moment, just long enough to find
her lips, and kiss her, walking her backwards, holding her,
guiding her, whisking her lips softly with his, the way she
had shown him.

The skies, radiant with sun just a few moments before,
suddenly darkened. A cloudburst released a torrent of rain.
They cried out in surprise, and started running.

Bali magic, she couldn't help thinking. An excuse, as if
they needed an excuse. A reason to hurry. Because she
could hardly wait.

Her feet moved so fast, she was agile as a child. She
could not feel the ground. It seemed as though the grace
that had come to her mainly through song was suddenly
conferred on her physically, and she'd become weightless,
literally enchanted, lifted on fairy wings. He ran close behind, his hand held ineffectually over her head, creating a

would-have-been umbrella that protected her not at all. And even as the rains drenched her clothes, she was already wet where the rains could not touch. Primed for his touch.

"You're soaked to the skin," he said on the porch of his little house, his tone, like his look, intense, grave. "We better get you out of those clothes."

What clothes she wore were flimsy: only the sarong tied over her bathing suit, clinging to her body, given some weight by the rain. He led her inside, grazed her bare shoulders with the palms of his hands, moving them to where the fabric was knotted, untying it, letting it fall to the floor. He reached behind her for the closing on her bathing suit top, eased her to a sitting posture on the edge of the bed, smiled as he heard the catch in her breath, on his face a look between pleasure and self-satisfaction. He kissed between her breasts, slowly, lingeringly, traced the tip of his tongue towards her heart.

"Lovely," he whispered. "I knew they'd be lovely. And sweet." He suckled her nipples.

More than a sigh escaped her. All the time since Charley's death she had felt tautly inert. The restraint she had not permitted herself to consider restraint but only what was decent, seemly, was unlaced like an old-fashioned corset from a too-voluptuous woman. Her flesh felt rippling, molten, overflowing onto his mouth, even as she ached for that mouth to do more.

His head moved toward her belly. His hair brushed her skin. She could see it, hanging, all of a golden piece, insinuating, hiding her from herself, a curtain between her and what was happening to her. And then sight disappeared, knowledge of where and who she was disappeared, and all became feeling, flame that danced on the head of a pin, as he moved down, and the tip of his tongue revived what had been dead in her.

Lazarus.

And when she cried out and moaned and wept with relief, he lifted her from beneath her knees and straddled her. She opened to him, closed around him. Remembered, as he cradled her hips in his powerful hands and pulled her down hard onto him, what it was like to have a man inside her, stretched and warmed and rocked in her hidden places. There was magic in her again, woman magic, loosed by a man. And Bali magic.

Even as she felt as if her heart would burst, and her insides would explode, that the force of her release would suffocate her, the naughty gods of Bali danced around the room and gave her heart, mind, body, *Air*. And, in the recesses of her soul, melody.

Tropical storms went along with the Christmas season in Bali. The rain falling that afternoon beat against the roof of Richard's hut, a relentless tattoo that calmed even as it cooled.

Not till afterward did she feel the humidity, the warm clamminess of his skin. She was reluctant to pull away, for fear he might think her discontented, dissatisfied. Since Charley's death she had lost track of everything but the longing, forgotten the actual elation, the physical exhilaration that came from the act of love. The remedy that was climax, a jolting reminder of what joy it was to be alive, flesh, human, an animal that could think, but at the same time suspend thinking and just be. Why couldn't she let it go at that?

She knew the answer even as she asked the question. Because it wasn't just sex. Not for her. It was coupling. Not simply coupling in the carnal sense, as a couple, but a joining with all that was out there. Infinite.

"Thank you," he whispered, his head on her chest. She reached for his hair, the moist, matted, but still silky feel of it. Pushed it back from his high, wide forehead and studied his face, the well-defined nose, the blemish on his mouth that seemed to make him even handsomer. His bright blue eyes made an appraisal of her. And she, in turn, made her own straightforward assessment, looking at his naked body directly for the first time.

The bones of his shoulders were very wide, a broadness emphasized by the definition. His shoulders and arms were muscular, amplified from the years of athletic activity, the forearms oversized, Popeye-like, moving down to his monumental hands. His waist was so slender as to seem almost feminine, an impression dispelled by the thickness of his thighs, and what lay between them. Naked, he seemed at once stronger and more vulnerable, the darkness of his tan edging the pale white triangle where his bathing suit had been. "You look sad," she said.

"I'm just wishing I had a way to rent us a villa. Just for one day. One night. But the best money came from the white-water rafting, and I . . ." Memory clouded his eyes. "I can't do that anymore."

She didn't ask why. In one of the rare instances of her life, Karen was putting a rein on her curiosity, at least the part that spoke it out. Her head was full of questions about him, but she was respecting his unwillingness to reveal too much. Either that, or she was really afraid to know. She understood he told her things as he was ready to, even the parts that might be lies.

His fingers circled her breasts, barely touching, palm turned outward, nails lightly grazing the surface of her skin. Lingeringly.

Afterplay. Many men loved you before, and all of them during. But few were those who took pleasure in loving you afterward. As though he had all the time in the world, and beyond it. No hurry. A satisfied smile on his face as he observed the effects of his handiwork.

"You're the most responsive woman I've ever been with," he whispered.

She didn't ask how many there were. Bad enough she had slipped deep into a vat of infatuation, without adding to the brew jealousy, possessiveness, especially about the past. The past was only a memory, she reminded herself from their early conversation, stopping short of the rest of the thought: that the future was a fantasy. The future seemed very real to her now, more solid, enriched by the prospect of a lover in it, the pillow next to hers no longer empty. The linen case that would cover it in her New York apartment would be meticulously pressed, like the sheets, fresh smelling.

"And the most giving," he said, and kissed first one, then the other breast. He lifted his head. "What can I give to you?"

"You've already given me a lot."

"I mean, something to drink. I've got some local grappa."

"Alcohol will only make me warmer."

"Not this. This will cool you off. From inside." He sat up and leaned across to a low credenza, took a crystal cordial glass from the top, reached inside, found a bottle of clear liquid, poured a little in a glass. He dipped the point of his tongue into the glass, and, barely touching the outside of her lips with his, pausing only to pry them open, insinuated his tongue into her mouth, ran the bracing flavor around her teeth.

It tasted sharp, licorice-y, cool. She welcomed the temperature and texture, took the tip of his tongue with her own, the heat of the room vanishing as she surrendered her whole self to his mouth. The eyes were the windows of the soul, according to the poet, but it seemed to Karen that the mouth was the gateway to the heart. So putting everything that was inside her, all she had to offer, all she was ready to receive, into the kiss, she reached for the deepest part of him, her own depths already dangerously engaged.

"You know, this isn't a camp in the Berkshires," Seth said when she got back to the villa. "They don't organize roller skating in the recreation hall when the weather sucks."

"You're right to be angry," she said, knowing it was true. "I'll make it up to you."

"We're leaving for Vermont?" he said.

"Why are you making this so hard for me?"

"Why weren't you here? This was supposed to be *our* holiday."

"I'm aware of that," Karen said. "I'm sorry."

"I took the hotel van to this old used bookstore on

Monkey Forest Road. I bought all these books of poetry, for your friend, on account of he's so *sensitive*."

"That was thoughtful of you."

"I figured maybe they would keep him busy, so I could have a little of your time. I met one of those dropout types, and he helped me pick them out. He knew a lot about your friend."

"I wish you'd stop referring to him as 'your friend.' He has a name."

"Yeah, well, maybe if I say 'your friend' enough you'll get how much your friend he isn't."

"But he is. He'd like to be your friend, too, if you'd give him a chance."

"Yeah? Well, this guy knew him well. And a *lot* about him. He used to take people white-water rafting."

"I know that."

"Did you know about the people who died because of him? Tourists he took on the river, who flipped out of the raft and got smashed against the rocks and drowned?"

"That could've happened to anybody," she said, defensively, understanding too much all at once, why the "White-Water Rafting" was crossed out on Richard's card, why he had said he couldn't do that anymore. Why his face drained of all color when he referred to it, even obliquely, as he always paled at anything that smacked of failure, loss, the specters that seemed to have chased him all the way to Bali. "It wasn't his fault."

"He told you that?"

"I just know."

"Like you know he isn't after your money. Like you know he isn't going to use you to get to the States."

"He doesn't want to leave here. He won't come with me."

"You've asked him?" Panic played on Seth's features.

"Not exactly," she said, knowing how close she'd come, knowing how much she wanted to, how ready she was to make plans. How quick to try to convert fantasy into a reality.

Seth got up from the bed, a look of consternation on his face. "God, Mom, you're supposed to be a mature woman."

"Well, maybe I'm not." Even as she said the words, she knew they were true, infuriated herself with how imprudent she was, her chagrin feeding into exasperation. "Maybe I'm just a lot older than I feel. Maybe maturity is overrated. I've had enough of being sane, and sensible. Maybe I see how little time there may be for falling in love."

"Falling into the sack, you mean."

She slapped him. Tears sprang to his eyes, stung hers.

"I'm sorry," he said, and started to cry. Childishly, little starts of sobs held back and then released, tears streaming down his cheeks, his nose starting to run. All pretense of sophistication was gone.

"I'm sorry, too." She started weeping with him,

ashamed of herself for losing her temper. She wiped his face with a tissue, put her arms around him.

They stood for a few moments like that, embracing, crying onto each other, because there was so much to regret. Death. The seeming inequity of life, who got to enjoy it and who didn't. Anger. Judgment. Loneliness. Fear of abandonment. The complexity of feelings people had for one another that they couldn't express with kindness and love.

She had a sudden shocking realization that it was a man she held, no matter how little boy his actions or his pronouncements were. She'd forgotten till that moment how big he was, his stature like that of his father's, making her reach up to hold him.

"I've been acting like such a smart-ass," Seth said, sniffling. "Dad always said, 'Nobody likes a smart-ass.'"

"I do," she said, and hugged him harder. "I do, with all my heart."

"God, you're so little," he said. "No wonder Dad had to take care of you."

There was a temple garden below the lobby terrace, a walled quadrant of unplanted earth with four stone statues, guardian spirits, draped with sarongs, as worshipers had to be. Every community in Bali, no matter what size—whether it was a cluster of houses belonging to one family,

descendants and in-laws, four generations living in a com-
pound, or a small village, or a great modern hotel—each
had its own temple.

Prayer and offerings were a part of the daily routine.
Flowers became their own art forms, arranged into miniature temples, sweet pink cookies and sour green apples ordered into towering pyramids, carried with effortless balance on beautiful heads, paraded alongside roads at different
hours of the day, as lace-bloused, sarong-wrapped, slender-
waisted women made their way to ceremonies, weddings,
cremations. Life-cycle rituals and celebrations were marked
with *penjors,* tall, decorated bamboo poles drooping palm
leaves, with curved upper ends, lining the streets like gala
question marks outside the houses where festivities took
place.

The temple garden at their hotel faced the sea, so standing in it, barefoot, as the respectful had to be, Karen could
hear the crash of the waves, counterpointing the music that
came from beside the lily pond, where musicians saluted
the twilight. They played flutes and drums, a *g'nender,* a
bright-sounding pipe that carried the melody.

She had found some incense by the opening in the wall
that led into the garden, left there for those who had not
come prepared, along with yellow sashes, without which
devotees were not supposed to enter a place of worship.
Although Karen did not know what the statues represented,
she lit four sticks of incense and placed one in the mouth-
like opening of each. Then she prayed to whoever the gods

were, and her own, that the people she loved would be happy, and kind to each other. She did not yet begin to hope, much less pray, that they could end up really liking each other, though the same part of her mind that bought new sheets flashed on that bright improbability.

"Now, there's a pretty picture," Richard said, from just outside the wall. He took off his sandals, wound a length of yellow rayon around the waist of his loose white trousers, and padded softly on the packed brown earth to where she stood.

"I'm not quite sure who I'm praying to," she said.

"Myself, I would speak to Saraswati," he said. "Consort of Brahma, goddess of knowledge, wisdom, and the arts. She must be very pleased to have you in Bali."

He brushed up against her, moved up close behind her, dancing against her back, insinuating his groin against her bottom. For a moment she thought she might be mistaken about what he was doing, that it was simply the proximity he wanted, affectionate, amiable. But then she felt the hardness, the pressure against her.

"Not here," Karen warned softly. It was nearly dark, but the temerity of the act, where they were, was overwhelming.

In a temple garden. Once past the amorous parked-car bumblings of her teenage years, her experience of love had always taken place in bedrooms. Charley had liked his comfort, familiar surroundings. Richard's movements against her, in the place they were, were as audacious as they were arousing. "Not here," she said again.

"It's an honored tradition in the great religions," he murmured, his hand moving slowly downward. "Students seduced by priests in temple gardens."

"You're a priest now?"

"A follower of the divine," he said, and turned her around. "You are divine. Love is divine."

He started kissing her. But these were different kisses. Neither the brusque ones of the beginning, nor the softly expert ones they had become with her tutelage. He was paying court to her now, subtly, lightly, giving respectful kisses. Curiously polite, especially considering the impudence of it, where they stood, what the rest of him was doing.

"O, Saraswati," he called out, not too loudly. He maneuvered Karen behind one of the statues, between the deity and the wall, pressed himself against her, lifting her sarong. *"Praise to you who are the giver of blessings, You who have the form of Desire."*

"What if someone comes?" she whispered.

"My intention exactly."

Six

"HOW ABOUT the Hard Rock Cafe?" Richard asked Seth at dinner. They were eating at Goa, a popular restaurant in Kuta, where one picked out fresh fish, huge lobsters from a display on beds of ice, and had them cooked to order. The restaurant had been Seth's choice. Richard had given him a list of options and his own recommendation, Made Warung, but Seth had bypassed whatever Richard suggested and picked from a guidebook.

"What about it?" Seth responded.

"Would you like to go there later? It's just down the street. Very lively, the young crowd."

"Hard Rocks are too noisy," said Seth. "My mom hates that kind of music."

"I don't hate it," Karen said. "I just worry about breaking my eardrums, and not being able to hear music that is music."

"Like her own," Seth said. "Have you heard her songs?"

"She's been very modest," said Richard. "I've asked, but she won't sing to me."

"I have a CD with some of her songs on it," Seth said. "I always travel with a bunch of CDs. I carry one of hers so she won't feel left out."

"Very generous." Richard said.

"He doesn't listen to it, though," Karen said. There was no displeasure or hurt in the comment, just an observation.

"It's not my style. A little too middle-of-the-road. But you'd probably like it. I'll lend it to you."

"I don't have a CD player," Richard said.

"I have one. Portable, with speakers. The one I was listening to on the beach. You have electricity?" There was a slightly imperious edge to the question.

"I have electricity."

"Well, it would be all right if you didn't. It also works on batteries. But I don't like to waste the energy. You can probably relate to that."

Although the tables in the restaurant were set widely apart, and the space the place occupied was vast, it still gave the impression of being crowded. Kuta itself was a village filled with crowds: tourists jamming streets already bottlenecked with hawkers; tourists complaining of how heavily trafficked and off-putting the place was, with fumes from countless motorcycles wiping out all scent of the sea;

tourists who said they would never come back to Bali, imagining that this was Bali; tourists who cursed Kuta but went there every night, because that was where the action was.

"So at last I shall hear your music," Richard said to Karen.

"They're really good songs if you don't mind *schmaltz*," Seth said.

"I'm afraid I don't know what that is."

"Sentiment," Karen said.

"Oh, it's more than sentiment," said Seth. "It's like . . . well, you know when someone's heart is too big, and they're all the time wearing it on their sleeve?"

"Actually, it's chicken fat," Karen said.

"Chicken fat can't kill you, unless it's in your arteries." Seth ate a forkful of whitefish. "But a heart that's too big . . ."

"Don't talk with food in your mouth," Karen said.

"The girl from the hotel who fancies you is at that table over there," said Richard. "She can't keep her eyes off you."

"Old Metal-Mouth?" Seth leaned over and waved to her. "Old No-Tits?"

"She'll have them one day," Richard said.

"But not within the next ten, which is all we have left," said Seth. "Besides, I thought you Buddhists were big on being in the moment."

"I'm not a Buddhist," he said, pronouncing it with a short *u* so that it sounded like *bud*.

"What exactly are you?"

"Searching."

"Me, too," said Seth, and pierced his fish. "For someone with really great tits."

Richard laughed.

"Don't encourage him." Karen said.

"The guidebook said this place had sexy lighting," Seth noted, as the young girl got up from her table and started toward theirs. "You consider this sexy, or is it just her?"

"Sex is in the eye of the beholder," Richard said.

"I thought that was beauty," said Seth.

"Well, what's sexy often seems beautiful."

"And more interesting than it really is," said Seth, looking at Richard pointedly, then checking from the sides of his eyes if his mother had caught his comment.

"G'day," the girl from the hotel said, grinning, at the side of his chair now, her braces catching the light.

"It's nighttime," Seth said.

"I know *that*. I only said 'G'day' because I thought it would make you laugh." She stood by the table shifting her weight from leg to leg.

"Would you like to join us?" Karen asked.

"Thank you, but I can't. I'm with my parents. I just wanted to say hello."

"Hello," said Seth.

"What's your name?" Karen asked.

"Jennifer." She had a heavy Australian accent so it sounded like "Jinifah."

Karen held out her hand. "I'm Karen. Seth's mother. And this is Richard."

"Hi." She turned unsurely toward Seth. "My parents wanted to know if you'd like to come with us to the Hard Rock Cafe."

"What a good idea!" Karen said to Seth. "You can have your fun and I can keep my eardrums."

"You want to get rid of me?"

"Nobody wants to get rid of you."

"We'd just like you to have a good time," insisted Richard.

"We *would* have a good time," Jennifer said. "Please?"

"Okay," Seth said grudgingly.

Her face lit up, and she all but clapped her hands. "I'll go tell them."

"See how easy it is to make a woman happy?" Richard said.

"I'm sure you do that all the time. In between leading travelers to their doom."

"What happened to the tears?" Karen put down her fork. "What happened to how sorry you were?"

"I have new things to be sorrier about," he said, and got up from his chair. "I think I'll go join people who want to be with me."

"Seth . . ." Richard said.

"Let him go," said Karen. "G'day."

You couldn't really hear at the Hard Rock Cafe. But Jennifer's parents took Seth aside and wondered aloud if that wasn't Richard Hensley his mother had been with. The Bramsons were not particularly exciting people, in Seth's opinion, but they did manage to infuse some enthusiasm into their curiosity.

"Wasn't that who she was with?" asked Jennifer's father, as they waited outside the men's room. It was the one wall in the packed place you could lean against and be cut off from the sound.

"You know him?"

"I know *about* him. Everybody knows *about* him. Took a bunch of Chinese tourists white-water rafting and they all ended up dead. He was the only survivor."

"Should have gone down with his raft, I guess," said Seth.

"Chinese government sent investigators." He was a slender man of indeterminate years, who had probably never looked young, his vacation clothes nondescript, khaki that would have looked muted even without his wearing it. "Thought it was a plot."

"What kind of plot?"

"To kill Chinese. You know, at the time of Sukarno when there was all the worry about the Chinese Communists taking over everything, the Balinese slaughtered thousands of Bali Chinese. Families who had been here for generations. Their own neighbors. Now with the economic crisis they're turning against the Chinese again all over Indonesia, because they've got the food shops. This is a very racist place, you know. They don't even like Australians."

"Why's that?"

Bramson shrugged. The door to the men's room opened, and a Japanese came out. Bramson waited till the man was out of earshot. "And they don't care for the Japanese, especially in large groups, which they always are."

"Go ahead," Seth said, indicating the bathroom.

"Thanks," said Bramson, and went inside.

"Oh, there you are," Mrs. Bramson said, peeking around the corner. "We were beginning to think you'd run off with some other girls."

There was a coyness, a cuteness to the way she said it that did not go with her appearance, which was curiously staid, even in Bermuda shorts. Seth had checked her out for breasts to see what Jennifer's prospects were, and found it discouraging.

"So where did your mother meet this Hensley?"

"They were introduced by the Dalai Lama."

"Really?"

The door opened and Bramson came out. "Excuse me," Seth said, and went into the bathroom.

"Seth isn't wrong," Richard told Karen. The two of them were on the covered porch of his little house, Karen in one of the big, low bamboo chairs with worn batik cushions, Richard leaning against a railing of bamboo as thick as logs. There was a waxing moon, nearly full, illuminating the chaos of wildflowers in the untended garden, hibiscus and Japanese ixora, delicate blossoms grown into clumps, like brilliant red snowballs. "I did lure travelers to their doom. I feel like a murderer."

"You didn't lure them. They wanted to go. You were only doing your job."

The light of the moon caught the slant of his cheekbones, the hollows beneath them, the slightly silvery glint of his hair in the muted glow. The scar on his mouth was obscured at that angle. His shirt, opened to the second button, revealed the Bali coin on its leather cord, above his nearly hairless chest. She touched him with her eyes, remembering how soft his skin was, holding in check her need to touch him with the rest of her.

"My *job*," he said. "Seth is right to feel contempt for me. In England I only hurt my father, my family. I was just a thief. All that was lost was money. But here, in Bali, six people are dead because of me."

"It was an accident. Accidents happen."

"So everyone said. But I should have been . . . what? More cautious? Less greedy. I'd done that trip a thousand times. I knew how treacherous it was. So hard to explain, you know, when you don't speak the language, 'Hold on when I say "bump." ' Maybe they didn't even know what bump was. Maybe the translator didn't tell them properly."

"What is bump?" she asked.

"When you come to the rocks, the boulders in the river, and see you're going to hit. I call out 'bump,' and they're supposed to hold very tight to the ropes. But the river was raging that day. Too full. Right after the rains. Nobody else would take them. Too dangerous. I should have called it off. But they were so eager. Penned up for all those years in China, let loose. With their pockets full of money."

"You *did* warn them?"

"I warned them. But I should have simply refused to take them. I wanted to go."

"So did they."

"I remember they were laughing, giggling like children, every time we hit. Fear does that, you know. Sometimes you confuse it with exhilaration." He ran his hand through his hair and turned towards her. "Just as one often confuses passion with love."

"Oh, stop trying to make what we have between us less than it is," Karen said angrily. "I know what I feel."

"Do you? Or do you feel what you feel?"

"What difference does it make? I'm happier now than I've been in I don't know how long." She got up from the chair and went to him, moved her hands, flat palmed against his well-toned, tight belly, up the front of his chest, feeling his skin through the silkiness of the cloth, bringing her fingers to rest on either side of his face, cupping his chin in her palms, drawing the wounded mouth toward her.

"But you *do* know how long it's been," he said softly, his lips not quite touching hers. "It's since you lost . . ."

"Charley," she said, and kissed him. And then whispered the name against his mouth. "Charley." And whispered it again. "At last I can say it without hurting."

"That's who you should be with. A man like Charley. A man who could really take care of you. I'm a spoiler. I poison everything I touch."

"Not me," she murmured, and moved his hand to her skin to better illustrate. "You haven't poisoned *me*."

He stroked her nonchalantly. "You great soft lump. With all you have, your energy, your talent, what do you want with me?"

"Pleasure. Life," she said. Closing her eyes, she gave herself over to the feelings he aroused in her. What did it matter if Richard was right and she only *felt*. Six people she hadn't known were dead, and even as she tried to digest the information, it meant nothing to her. It was so foreign to her experience, it couldn't touch her, as he could. Like reading in the papers about Kosovo.

What did faraway deaths mean to her, when stacked up against the close, sweetly blistering truth that she was once again alive? Feeling how much more the world seemed, viewed, tasted, experienced with a partner. She reached up to kiss Richard. She felt happy. That was what it was about, wasn't it? Weren't you meant to be happy?

"We'd best go inside," he murmured.

"My feelings exactly."

"Whatever else this is," he said, "it's pretty sexy."

They were not quite in the door when he was already halfway out of his trousers, dancing on one foot, the curve of his buttocks ivory in the moonlight, his erection taking on its own luminosity, a beacon to her. She backed into the room, stripping herself of what little clothing she wore, what few defenses she still had.

The temple at Besakih, known as the Mother Temple, was approached by a well-maintained road, bypassing the dangers that pilgrims had faced in the past, hazardous ravines, dense forests, the steep climb up the slopes of Mount Agung. Karen had asked Richard if he would act as their driver and guide, hiring an an air-conditioned van to take them on the arduous journey. The impasse between mother and son with respect to Richard's presence as a suitor had remained an impasse, but his acting as their guide was acceptable to Seth, since that was what Richard did for a living. "I'd like to see what exactly he does," Seth had murmured under his breath.

The excursion had been Seth's idea. He had had enough hotel, and ocean, and pool, and Hard Rock, he'd complained. They were in Bali, he reminded Karen; he'd seen precious little of Bali. Armed with his guidebook, he'd selected Besakih as their first major outing. He'd climbed rather excitedly into the van beside Richard, who told him he'd be able to see better from up front.

They drove to and through Ubud, the main art colony of the island, passed roadside craft shops, displays of woven carpets, quilts. Little wooden signs hung from carven gates: "Healer," "Magic."

"Can we stop for some magic?" Seth asked Richard.

"It's black magic," Richard said. "You don't want to get into that."

"How do you know?" Seth asked. "What exactly is it?"

"Bringing harm to your enemies."

"I'm too young to have enemies," Seth said.

"The whole history of this place is fraught with good magic and amazing tales," Richard said. Sometimes on his tours, Richard would tell a story about Bali, how, when the Dutch invaded Indonesia in the early part of the twentieth century, it seemed such a quaint little island that for a while they left it alone. He told it to Seth and Karen and about how one day a great Dutch merchant ship foundered on the coral reefs. After it had sunk, and settled, the Balinese swam out and farmed it for treasures.

So the Dutch, having the excuse they needed, took their warships to the shores of Bali, with their guns and their cannons, demanding surrender. But the rajas, the kings of the villages, along with their families and followers, appeared in all their splendor, wearing silks and golds, and started throwing their jewelry at the Dutch, giving them what they thought they wanted. When the invaders would not go away or retreat, the Balinese took their ancient knives, as if they would go with them against the sophisticated weapons. But instead they killed themselves, their children, their families.

And so it went all over the island. Someone took pictures. They were circulated throughout the rest of the world, giving rise to such indignation that the Dutch had no choice but to withdraw. The culture of Bali was declared so "unique" that an ordinance was passed decreeing that it should stay as it was, free from settlements, free from missionaries. That story was taught in many great religions, Richard always told his listeners on the tours, as an example of sacrifice that had saved a civilization. Proof that human nature could ennoble itself for the sake of an ideal, an idea, honor. So the gods of Bali were preserved.

"You think it was worth everybody dying?" Seth asked.

"I've never really understood the idea of sacrifice," Richard said. "It seemed a bit silly to me. Not to mention suicidal."

Rice paddies laced with shoots of bright green bordered the sides of the road. Tiny, slim women with logs on their heads, washtubs loaded with coconuts, steadied with only a lightly placed hand, shifted slender hips as they walked to their destinations with their barely acknowledged burdens.

"Awesome," Seth said, looking out the window. "How do they do that?"

"Every Bali woman can do it," said Richard. "From the time they're little girls. When you climb back up to the road from the river after . . ."—he paused—". . . after white-water rafting, there're five-year-old girls on the steps with washtubs on their heads, carrying cold sodas for the tourists."

They had packed themselves a picnic lunch, with sandwiches from the food store across from the hotel, and fruit. Richard had brought along a cooler filled with soft drinks.

"You know anything about where we're going?" Seth asked, turning toward Karen as he chewed, washing it down with Coke.

"A little."

"Mount Agung," Richard said, "where Besakih is, is supposed to have incredible power. Why don't you read us what I marked in your guidebook, Seth."

Seth opened the book, found the page, cleared his throat, and started to read aloud: " 'Far more alarming than the physical perils were the psychic risks of abandoning the world where humans belong to approach the supernatural realm of the spirits.' Cool. I can hardly wait."

"In 1963," Richard said, "there was a tremendous volcanic eruption. A major celebration they only have once every hundred years. Sukarno, the president at the time . . ."

"He was a bad guy, right?" Seth asked.

"Maybe not when he started," said Richard. "But power does funny things to people, especially when they have the key to the treasury. Anyway, he wanted to go to Besakih with a group of his diplomats. So he had the priests switch the dates to make it convenient for them, and right in the middle of the ceremony there was this *enormous* eruption. Lava. Thousands of people wiped out. Talk about displeasing the gods. They must have really been angry. But politics will do that."

"I used to consider going into politics," Seth said. "But not anymore."

"So what *do* you want to do?" Richard asked him.

He was quiet for a moment. "Win."

The steamingly hot climb up to the temple from the parking lot, on seemingly endless steps, continual rises, was to Karen like a mountain hike for which she was totally unprepared. "Come on, Mom," Seth urged her, taking her elbow. "You can do it. You're not *that* out of shape."

"Thank you," she managed to say. Perspiration streamed down her face, her neck, from between her sarong-surrounded legs, soaking the socks she wore with her sneakers, a lucky last-minute choice instead of sandals.

"Remember, you don't *feel* old."

"Don't tease me," she said, climbing. "I can hardly breathe."

"Poor Mom," he said, with genuine sympathy. His voice became infused with energy. "You can do it. I have faith in you. You'll feel great when you get to the top, and all this is behind you."

"How long do you think that will be?"

"How much farther is it, Richard?" Seth asked.

"Not far," Richard said.

It was far. By the time they reached the temple and she saw there were still more steps to climb among the vast complex of smaller temples, Karen felt faint.

"You want to rest?" Richard asked.

"Rest you can do when you've faded," said Seth, and held her arm. "Come on. You're doing great. I'm proud of you, Mom. You're a regular mountain goat."

Finally, they were in a courtyard. "The landing field of the gods," Richard said.

"Thank them for me." Karen sat down as best she could, in a triangle of shade. She was dressed in a yellow lace blouse the housekeeper at the hotel had loaned her, with a red sarong striped with gold wound around her hips and legs, secured at the waist by safety pins, belted with a yellow sash. She had struggled all through the climb to keep ease of movement in her legs, the sarong bound so tightly around them she felt her knees would lock. Richard had made a gentle show of holding her arm, not so forcefully as to seem that she couldn't make it on her own, which she silently thought she wouldn't. She wondered how the Balinese women managed to walk with the grace they did, much less climb, with their movements so compromised. Tourism, like love, demanded devotion, serious commitment.

When she was able to continue, Richard led them to a second courtyard. Beyond the gilt-painted, heavily decorated *bales,* three raised lotus thrones rose like pyramids. Richard took his shoes off, eased himself to his knees, bowed his head. Then he signaled to Seth to do the same.

"Are you really praying?"

"It's a sign of respect," Richard said.

"We're supposed to take our shoes off?" Seth asked, alarmed, looking around at the dirt on the stones.

"I will if you will," Karen said.

They took off their shoes and knelt beside Richard. He looked up and pointed to the three empty thrones. "Wisnu, Siva, Brahma," he pointed. "The great gods of Bali."

"Who sits where?" asked Seth.

"Anyone sits anywhere they want to," Richard said. "That's real power."

"It's kind of inspiring, really," Seth said. "All these prayerful people." Groups of villagers were clustered around, some collecting holy water, some giving offerings of food and flowers, paying respects, as Richard had explained, completing rituals for the dead. "Maybe that's what I'll be when I'm older."

"Prayerful?" Karen asked.

"One of the gods," said Seth.

Richard preceded them down into the tunnel, assuring them there were lit torches all along the way and that he'd be in front of them, in case they tripped. Seth hesitated.

"I'm scared," he said, outside the entry, in a hushed voice.

"We don't have to go into it if you don't want to," Karen offered.

"I don't mean about the tunnel." He looked suddenly very young, big as he was, very much her little boy. "I mean about life. I'm really not sure what I'm supposed to be." The wiseacre was gone from his voice, from his face, from his attitude, all the uncertainty he had spent so much time keeping hidden in the guise of smart aleck suddenly glaringly visible.

"I thought for a while it was going to be football. But that went with the coach, and not having Dad. No father to set me an example of how to *become* anything."

"Your father was a good and decent man and loving man. He worked very hard."

"For what? To die young? Who do I have left for an example? The president?" A look of sorrow passed over his face, a teenage version of a nation disappointed. "And I

can't take my example from a . . ."—he paused for a moment—"a ne'er-do-well."

He looked away, golden lashes fanning eyes empty of
anger, sensitive to the hurt his words might be inflicting.
"It's nothing personal, Mom. I don't really dislike him.
He's fun. Actually, we sort of get along. But I'm afraid to
hang out with Richard."

It was the first time Seth had actually said his name to
her. "Why?" she asked.

"If I was with him a lot, *he's* what I'd become. A bigger
version of me. A kid who doesn't know what he's supposed
to be, who might never be *anything*.

"That's part of what made me so mad. It wasn't just
that I was jealous—you were supposed to be spending your
vacation with *me,* so I know that was a lot of it. But what I
really couldn't stand was how much he reminded me of
myself. I mean, he told me all that crap he must have told
you about Bali being a mirror. He's kind of a mirror of *me*.
What I could be if I never found the handle, and became
nothing."

There was little Karen could say, to him or to herself.
To live for love, to live for feeling was a luxury. She had
come to a point in her life when she might be entitled to
those. But to set them as a goal for her son?

This was Bali. Eden. Any moment the dream would
come to an end, and with that would come reality, the
need for commitment, purpose, the toughness of a world
that demanded a man be a man. Whatever that meant.

"That's what really scares me." Seth said. "It isn't only you I'm afraid for, Mom. It's me."

They were into the tunnel, catching up with Richard, following him down into the temple's structural core, where, according to the guidebook, deities, ancestors, and spirits descended on festive occasions to take their places in the shrines. Richard stepped aside to let Seth and Karen pass.

"But, then again, maybe I'm not thinking lofty enough," Seth said. "I mean, the whole point of Bali is that life is holy. You're supposed to find out how holy it is, right? To get to the best place you can get inside yourself. So why couldn't we just hang out with the gods? What's to stop us from becoming one of them?"

"I think they're already firmly established."

"Well, so was God, right?" Seth was starting to talk very fast now, the way he had when he was a little boy and had only recently found ways of putting into words the thoughts he was beginning to have in his head, language pouring out of him, the excitement that came from connection and discovery lending him a kind of radiance. Now it was all combining with the energy, the rush of being sixteen.

"But then Jesus came, and told everybody he was 'the way.' And what he was the way to was God. And the kingdom of Heaven was within, and all that. So why isn't everybody God?"

"Maybe they are," Karen said. "Maybe they just don't know it."

"Maybe I can teach them." He put his guidebook in his backpack, now that they were descending to a place too dark to read, the flickering torch attached to the wall giving them almost no light. "Maybe that's what I can be is a teacher."

He turned to her and smiled, angelic, just before the tremor struck. "Till I trade it in for becoming one of the gods."

When the earth moves, there is little to hold onto. Not just physical shifts occur. What has been fixed in our thinking, our certainty that there are some things we can count on, like the ground beneath our feet, is literally undermined.

It began with a rumble that sounded like a far-off cry of pain, a bellow so deep and so anguished, a prehistoric creature might have been trapped in the recesses of the tunnel, in agony. For a moment, Karen imagined that a phrase she had never quite understood and always disliked, "the bowels of the earth," was now grim in its accuracy, and the bowels were in an uproar, gaseous, unable to pass whatever was blocking them. The walls of the tunnel began to vibrate, just a little at first, so that it might have seemed a momentary blur of vision, dust from the hard-packed dirt

on either side softening the air like a haze. And then the
jolt hit, an angry shock. Karen lost her footing, and fell.
Seth reached for her, but in the violent motion they could
not catch each other's hands. Far below, people screamed.
Torches were shaken from their mountings, crashed to the
ground, extinguished. They were in darkness.

Somewhere behind her, Karen could hear Richard calling to them frenziedly over the uproar, the cracking of
rock, the falling stones. Something struck her on the rump,
terrifying in the moment, because of the circumstances.
But in the silence that followed, she realized it had seemed
quite like a hand, delivering a whack to her bottom, chastising but not really punishing. "Seth?" she called, her first
concern her son. "Seth?"

He did not answer. "Oh, God," she cried out. "Seth?"
Her beautiful boy. The blossom of her soul. All that was left
of Charley. All that truly mattered to her in the world, she
knew quite clearly in that eerie hush. Seth, who thought
he'd been set aside, put in second place, runner-up to her
passion.

"Oh, God, please," she murmured to herself, a torrent
of guilt and fear washing over her. She shifted her body and
got to her knees. "Please," she whispered, and prayed, and
promised, and swore that if Seth were all right, if they got
out of this alive, Richard would be out of her life forever.

Bonny Prince Richard, setting his course on such careless, carefree seas, carrying her along, making her seem to forget her prime obligation, the first order of her trust, her only son. Making Seth believe she had forgotten about him, which she *never* had: She had only been momentarily diverted. That's all Richard had been, a diversion, making her as empty-headed as the other women he'd been with, living for her heart. And not even really her heart. Just what made that heart beat faster. Blood aroused. Lust. The addictiveness of desire satisfied.

This was her comeuppance, for not holding fast enough to her duty to her son. "Oh, please," she murmured against the backs of her hands, held to her mouth in prayer, half stifling her words, beseeching them to go higher, reach a power that could change things. "I'll give Richard up. Only let Seth be all right."

The rescuers were a long time in coming. The air in the tunnel was thick with dust. A torch, scrambled for and relit by Richard, showed the entry to be blocked, as was the passage in front of them. Richard kept touching her, trying to hold her, steady her, comfort her. But she pulled away.

"Seth?" Karen called out, over and over, through the rocks that had fallen in front of her, barring the way. Obliterating him? "Seth?"

"Mom?" she heard, at last. The deep but somehow still

quavering voice, so recently changed to a man's voice. The child's voice had been strangely even deeper, a gravelly basso that made everybody laugh, so out of place was it in a little boy. It echoed now in her memory, shaking her to her core. She was so grateful to hear it again, in its present tone. Not surprisingly, strong as the voice was, it sounded uneven, trembling as the earth had been.

"Are you okay?"

"I think," he said, from beyond the rocks. "Are you?"

"I'm fine," she said, and closed her eyes, whispered a soundless "Thank you," swore she would ask nothing more for herself.

It was night by the time they were rescued. Men had dug with their hands and primitive tools to free them.

"The gods must be very angry," Richard said, in a kind of uneasy jest, when they had at last reached the van. "I'm so glad you're both all right. Please," he said to Karen, reaching for her. "Sit beside me."

"I'll sit in the back with my son," she said coldly.

Seven

ETH WAS SILENT during the long ride back to
Denpasar. Karen had her arm around him—there was
no way she could hold him too close now. He did not seem
to be sleeping. His face was drained, his full lower lip pulled
up into an almost invisible line by the grip of his top front
teeth, so the slightly disappointed pout that so touched her
was not in evidence.

"Are you all right?" she asked him.

He looked up at her. His face was just below her shoulder, the slump of his posture, the experience of the afternoon having allowed him to relax back into being her son,
with none of the distancing that came between mother and
teenager. He moved closer and whispered, so that only she
could hear him: "I saw Dad."

"What?"

"I saw him. In the tunnel. When the quake hit. I saw him like I'm seeing you."

"You were in shock," Karen said. "We got shaken up. Literally."

"No question," he said. "But Dad was there."

She did not allow Richard to embrace her, even in a friendly fashion, when they got back to the hotel. "Thank you for getting us back safely," she said, archly. "I'll just go get my money and pay you for your services."

"You don't have to pay me," he said, a wounded expression on his face.

"You were acting as an employee, and you will be paid," she said.

He looked bewildered. "Do we have to take care of it right now? Can't I come back tomorrow?"

"As you wish. Good night." She started to close the door.

He stopped it with his hand. "Why are you angry at *me?* I didn't cause the earthquake. It was probably Siva, the god of destruction."

"We shouldn't have come to a place where people worship a god of destruction."

"Destruction is also transformation," Richard said.

"I've had enough of your lore," she said, and shut the door.

She put Seth to bed, tucked him in, as she hadn't since he was a boy. "What was that about Dad being in the tunnel?" she asked him.

"You know how they said in the guidebook, about the tunnel being used by ancestors and spirits? Well, Dad was there. He was right in my face. Remember how he used to tell me to get out of his face? Well, he got right into mine."

"A lot of things happen in your mind when you're in shock," Karen said. "You must have been imagining."

"I wasn't imagining. The guidebook talked about the psychic powers there."

"Maybe you had a little too much guidebook. Maybe the combination of the stuff in the book, and being scared . . ."

"It was Dad," he said. "Trust me. And he told me . . ."

"You heard him?"

"Not out loud. But I heard him. He told me I should be more loving to you, and understand your needs."

She smiled and hugged him. "That sounds like your Dad, all right."

"Then you believe me?"

"I believe we've both been through an ordeal. Ordeals make you very suggestible." Then she remembered the smack to her bottom, and wondered if it could have been

Charley. Chastising but not punishing, it had felt. What Charley would have done. A good swift smack to her spiritual rear, for falling so far behind in what really mattered.

The telephone rang. She picked it up. It was Richard, cajoling, pleading, needing to know how she was, why she was angry with him. "I'd really appreciate it if you didn't call me, Richard." She hung up the phone.

As Seth had watched her all along—plummeting into this relationship, saving the menu from her first lunch with Richard, along with the napkins from their cocktail dates, and paper umbrellas from their drinks—he regarded her behavior on the way back from Besakih and her hanging up on Richard with more than slight misgivings. He had observed his mother turning into a fellow high schooler before his very eyes, all but waiting for her invitation to the prom, the corsage that would come from it pressed into a memory book, along with the menu and napkins. So to see her showing what seemed outright antagonism toward Richard alarmed him.

"Shouldn't you call him back? What if he can't sleep?"

"Stay out of it," Karen said. "You be the son. I'll be the mother."

He could hear her turning restlessly in her bed during what was left of the night. He himself found sleep elusive, the specter in the tunnel rearing up inside his head. To his relief, his father's face was as it had been when he was still robust, handsome, strong, without the sunken cheeks, the glazed eyes, the weakened chin that had ravaged him with his illness. Seth had been unsure about the possibility of an afterlife, since the one on earth seemed so unpredictable and out of balance, so many villains going unpunished, bombs missing Saddam Hussein, but cancer striking down his dad. So to see his father's spirit manifested in its healthy human form, not as it had been in death, was a source of consolation, in addition to the wonder. And fright. He did not mean to leave out the fright.

He had known right away that his father was displeased with him. The face had been unsmiling, disapproving, as when Seth would bring home a bad report card. Even before the words sounded in his head, he knew from his father's look that he was being reprimanded, that he had done something wrong. When he heard that he should be more loving to his mother, and understand her needs, he grasped at once that he had not been loving toward her at all, thinking exclusively about his own wants. The message had ended with what seemed in Seth's head a sonic boom: *"Remember!"* In retrospect (one of his favorite expressions, which he used from time to time when he considered becoming a historian), he realized that the encounter had been an extremely positive one, since it would have been in order, and in character, for his father to give him hell. That he had glowered only a bit fiercely, made a suggestion that was not quite an order, and told Seth not to forget what he'd said showed that he had evolved in the hereafter. Apparently temper died along with the body.

Little by little the fear in Seth receded. The terror he had felt during the earthquake in the tunnel, the sense of dread he'd experienced at seeing his father's visage, all of it now seemed beside the point. If life was not over when it was over, there was nothing to be afraid of, since the worst that could happen on this side was that you could die.

But now a new worry arose in him: His mother might never again be happy. She had bloomed with Richard's attention, her color high, the light in her eye restored, her step and attitude jaunty, the aging, which her husband's illness and death had added, stripped away. But like a jerk, which he thought of himself now as being, Seth had made it hard on her. His biggest anxiety after his father's funeral, anxiety that tripped along hand in hand with the lead-footed grief, was that he, as the only man in her life, would not be able to give her what she needed. And the moment she found someone who seemed able to, he'd gotten mad.

In trying to cope with his father's death right after it had happened, Seth read a lot of books about the afterlife and near-death experiences. None of them mentioned that people came back from The Light and gave up their boyfriends. He could only guess that her ordeal in the tunnel had made her decide to abandon what was frivolous. But if sex and courtship were frivolous, if Richard was frivolous, (as Seth still suspected he was, but his assignment was to consider his mother's needs, *remember!*) the frivolity had obviously made her feel better, lightened her load. Even as she slept, now, fitfully, punching her pillows, tossing, Seth could feel her heaviness returned, the squeak of chalk on the blackboard of her life irritating her.

It was his fault; he knew it. His first action in the morning would be to make Richard his friend, welcome him to their circle. A generous gesture, no question. But even as he contemplated his own magnanimity, a word he could still not pronounce aloud, he realized that it might be fun to have a buddy. Exceptional as Karen was, besides being his mother, she *was* a woman. And the truth, the very deep truth, as Seth knew it now, and knew it to be all right, even approved of by his father, was that he liked Richard. Liked him a lot.

Birds sing a different kind of song in Bali. As their heads are more daintily shaped and colorful than those of their sparrow cousins in the West, so the chirp that they sound at dawn's striping the sky is lighter in tone, more melodic, a whistle version of the gamelan perhaps.

They fluttered around the courtyard outside the room, some in their hummingbird-like holding pattern, seeming to hover, rather than fly, above the flowers. There were wooden doors one could draw shut, inside the sliding glass that led to the patio, closing out the light, muting the warbling. But Karen had always left them open so that the day, with its bright luster, the thick tropical foliage, was the first thing she would see on opening her eyes.

This morning, though, what she saw was Richard, his nose pressed against the glass like the hungry little girl at the bakery window in the children's tale. One hand shaded his eyes in an effort to see into the room. He was in his cutoffs and sandals, a T-shirt clearly outlining his chest, which seemed to give the lie to the boy she now perceived him to be, by Seth's appraisal, which even as it forgave, underlined the similarity between them. The episode in the tunnel had reduced her to a level of judgment close to ridicule, not only of herself, but of all she had prized, except her son.

She put on a short robe, and not even bothering to brush her hair or her teeth, opened the glass doors and stepped outside, shutting them behind her. "Yes?"

"Yes?" he said, his cocky expression banished, leaving confusion, hurt. "I'm up all night, and that's how you greet me? 'Yes'?"

"Well, what do you want?"

"What's happened to you?"

"Reality," she said. "In a crisis, things become clear."

He reached for her, but she backed away. "It's over," she said.

"You can't be serious. It took this . . . *awful* thing to make me realize how much I care about you. It couldn't have turned you the other way round."

"But it did. You were right. I was confusing attraction with love. I don't really love you."

He blanched beneath his tan. "But what if I love you?"

"You'll get over it," she said. "You're young." She started to open the doors back into the villa.

"Don't you even care what I accomplished? That I've been working on getting us a place to be alone in, with air-con? That I've almost achieved my ambition?"

"It's good to know you have one," she said. "Good-bye."

"Without so much as a kiss?"

"I haven't brushed my teeth," she said, her back to him. "I always wonder at those stories where lovers wake in the morning, and kiss, without brushing their teeth. No sense of reality, anymore than I had."

She went inside. Seth, hidden in the corner, ear close to the door, sprinted into the bathroom, came out of it pretending that was where he had been.

"Are you finished in there?" she said.

"Sure. You can go in." He waited till the door was closed, and pulling a pair of shorts on over his underwear, opened the door and took off after Richard, who was making his slump-shouldered way toward the beach. "Hey! Wait up!" he called. "Richard!"

The Englishman turned. He seemed surprised at seeing Seth running toward him.

"She doesn't mean it," Seth said, catching up with him,

slightly out of breath. "It's my fault. She thinks she's doing it for me. I've been kind of jealous."

"Not really," said Richard, blandly.

"She thinks I don't like you. But I do."

"You do?"

"Your average near-death experience will do that. I mean, once they dig you out, you feel a genuine sense of fondness for your fellow fellows." He put his arm around Richard's shoulders and started walking with him.

"So I'm on your side now," Seth continued, stopping short of telling him about the ghost. That part was too intimate, something that had to stay between Seth and Charley and Karen. It was one thing to share having had a near-death experience, another to say what you had seen in the way of a phantom father. Especially as a stranger, which this man still really was, might think you were nuts. "You do really care for my mom, don't you?"

"I do," said Richard. "I do indeed."

"Then all we have to do is show her we're becoming friends, and it'll be okay."

There were boogie boards for rent everywhere on the beach, next to tiny, open, thatched-roof restaurants with tables on the sand, huts with young women giving manicures, painting flowers on tourist toes. The smell of powerful spices, along with smoke, blew from open braziers, where picnicking Bali families barbecued fish. From somewhere close by came the crisp aroma of roasting pig, for a feast that evening of *Baba Guling*, at one of the hotels. Kites flew. Hawkers peddled paintings of the *Ramayana*, the Hindu tale, a part of *The Mahabarata*, made into a ballet performed almost nightly at numerous places in Bali. It was a favorite of the locals as well as tourists, combining as it did the erotic and a drama of good and evil, kidnapped princesses and wicked-masked gods and demons, dancing among chattering monkeys, played by local men, muscular brown torsos naked to their well-hewn waists. They wore black and white checked trousers, the same fabric and pattern of the sarongs that modestly draped religious statues and sometimes even the lower parts of trees. The white symbolized good, the black evil, both forces prayed to in Bali, the one invited, the other begged to stay away. But both were honored, since the presence of the two was considered necessary for balance in the world.

Balance on a surfboard, however, was not as easily or symbolically achieved. Seth had gone with Richard to his little house near the beach where they'd picked up a surfboard for Seth's first lesson, and from there to the beach. Before they began, Richard made Seth douse himself with protecting sun cream.

"Your mother would never forgive me if you got burned again," Richard said.

"I won't get burned," Seth said, spreading the cream. "And she's going to forgive you."

They started on the beach, on the sand, the board lying flat a few feet from the water, as Richard instructed Seth how to position himself. His arms were over the sides on the sand, where they would be when he was in the ocean.

"Now you paddle free style," Richard said, kneeling beside the board, "till you get to the place where you wait for the wave. When you feel the swell start to come, you take hold of the rails . . ."

"I don't see any rails," said Seth.

"The sides of the board are called rails. You hold onto them, push up, get to your knees, and stand . . ."

"I can do this," Seth said, getting to his feet, already bored. "Let's go in the water."

"You get up like that, you're down."

"I've known some surfers. They're not too heavy on mentality. And I'm a natural athlete. A skier."

"It isn't about mentality. And those other things will help you a little, but not entirely. This is a sport like no other. It's about knowing how to wait. You have to read the wave, follow it, but not get crushed by the strength. You need to observe, and feel, follow which way it's going. Watch it come and go, like the seasons."

"Less talk, more action," Seth said impatiently.

"You can't rush this, anymore than you can the wave. Anymore than what's coming to you in life. You can't push the river."

"How about the ocean?"

Richard ignored the attempted parry. "You also need confidence. Confidence in yourself."

"I'm covered on that one." He held his arms out, balancing them on the air, imitating the motions he'd seen surfers make on the water.

"There's a difference between confidence and braggadocio."

"Whoa!" Seth exclaimed, stopping the mock surfing. "There's a million dollar word. What's it mean?"

"When you bluster. When you brag. When you act like you're sure of yourself but you're really not."

"You don't think I'm sure of myself?"

"I think you have every right to be," said Richard. "You have everything going for you, but you're not really sure you do. So you often seem too proud. Some people see that as arrogance."

"Is that what happened to you?" Seth asked.

"I suppose so. In a way."

"Which way?" Seth asked.

"Every way," said Richard. "Let's put on your leash." He took the tubing from the end of the board, closing it with velcro around Seth's ankle. "You need this so you don't lose the board. You've got to be responsible . . ."

"I'm highly responsible."

". . . because the board is like a weapon," Richard continued, undeterred. "Like a spear. If it gets away from you and gets caught in the current, it could kill somebody." The blood seemed to drain from beneath his skin,

as the thought of someone being killed appeared to reso-
nate through him. Guilt played across his face.

"I'm ready." Seth lifted the board, heading for the water. "I'm a natural athlete, I'm responsible, I'm confident,
and I won't make the mistake of being too proud."

"Well, you can try," said Richard. "But the ocean will
knock it out of you."

"This really sucks," said Seth, his mouth full of water,
eyes reddened from the salt, cheeks colored from the sun,
with an overlay of mortification. "Why don't we just go for
a hike?"

"Once you've got it, it'll be a part of your nature."

"I like nature to be Nature." He lifted himself back
onto the board, belly down, legs trailing in the water. "The
feel of the ground under my feet. Let's go smell some trees
instead of this cruddy salt."

"When it all comes together, you'll know exactly what
to do. You'll get hypnotized by it. You'll be riding with the
gravity pull of the moon, moving with the tides. It's addic-
tive."

"I don't want to get addicted to anything," Seth said.

"But you *do* want to win. And you can. And then it'll
be like a second language."

"I'm still working on the first one," Seth said, in position now, his belly on the board. "Braggadocio. Where'd

you get that one?" He pushed himself up, got to his knees, cautiously managed to stand, half crouched, balanced, for several seconds steady on his feet. "I did it! I got it!" he cried, before the board slipped from underneath and he toppled back into the water.

He came up sputtering. "I did it for a minute, anyhow," he said. "So I'm entitled to a little braggadocio."

"When you get it, you won't need braggadocio." Richard reached for the board, held it till Seth got a grip. "You'll have the real thing."

"You make it sound like surfing is noble." He raised himself up again in the center of the board, threw his legs up behind him.

"It is if it teaches you patience." Richard said. "Patience is something that whether or not you want to, you learn."

Seth stood, and slipped. "Go fuck yourself," he managed to say before he hit the water.

"What a great guy Richard is." Seth sat in the tub in his bathroom, soaking off the salt and the aches he did not mention to Karen. "I don't mean good. I mean *great*. He has amazing patience. It's hard to understand why you don't like him anymore."

"I never said I didn't like him." She stood at the sink, putting on her makeup.

"Then why are you dumping him?"

"Why did you stay away so long? Did it ever occur to you I might be worried?"

"You're always worried. You like to worry."

"That isn't true," said Karen.

"Then why worry? It's not like worry changes anything. You should be having fun. Don't you want to be with him?"

"There's no point."

"It doesn't have to have a point. It's a holiday. You're supposed to leave your cares behind. You're only young once." He smiled. "Except of course in your case. You look really great for someone that old."

"Is that supposed to make me feel good?"

"It's the truth."

"Women don't like to hear the truth about age." She closed her mascara brush. "I'll meet you on the terrace. There's a Christmas party."

"I forgot it was even Christmas, it's so un-Christmasy here," Seth said.

"I have a present for you." Karen went to her suitcase and took out a sloppily wrapped package, the ribbon badly tied. She looked at it curiously. "Have you already opened this?"

"Well, I needed to make sure you still really loved me, and bought me a good present." He grinned and kissed her, reopened the package. "It's a great watch, Mom. Waterproof. Cool. I can wear it surfing. I have a present for you, too." He reached into the bottom of his bag and drew out a big square box.

She unwrapped it, smiling. It was a framed, signed lead-sheet of a song by Irving Berlin, "When My Dreams Come True." "Oh, this is wonderful," she said. "I didn't even think you knew who Irving Berlin was."

"I didn't. The guy at the shop told me."

"Thank you." She kissed him. "It's the perfect present."

"Do we have something for Richard?"

"I want you to forget about Richard."

"But he's a really great guy. He's my bud. Can I invite him to the party?"

"You most certainly cannot." She switched out the light above the mirror.

"These are great hors d'oeuvres," Seth said. "A shame that on Christmas we can't share them with the needy."

"Richard isn't needy." Karen sat down on the stone wall bordering the terrace, away from the other guests. "Why are you spending so much time with him?"

"He's great company."

"He's a very manipulative man. But I didn't think he'd try to manipulate you."

"He's not. I'm the one who went after him."

"Are you all that anxious to learn to surf?"

"I guess it might really feel good, once you know how to do it."

"You don't sound very enthusiastic. Why are you spending all this time on something you're not even sure you like?"

Seth thought about the ghost, what it had instructed him, wondered whether to speak of that again. But she didn't seem to believe he had really seen his father. If she didn't like the idea of being manipulated by a man, how would she feel about a spirit trying to control from the beyond?

Better to make it his own problem, Seth thought; she was open to helping him with those. He looked past the palm trees, where a light lit up a portion of beach, beyond it a long patch of ocean, glittering black, mirroring the moon. He narrowed his eyes. "I don't like to be beaten," he said. And heard the truth of it.

He went to sleep early so he could wake when the water was calm, as he'd noted it the first time a few moments after dawn, when he'd still been upside down in time. There was a light gray sheen to the sea, as though it had been silver plated. He ran on the cool sands, the tide that had just gone out leaving it satiny beneath his soles, the usually grating texture absent, as were waves in the sea. It looked like a pond, really, a pond that stretched to the horizon, the whitening sky to the west blending with the line of sea. Then the sun rose higher in the east, and changed it into different blues: the sky azure, as Jim Morrison would have put it, the water aquamarine. Seth jogged along the edge, a whisper of foam playing between his toes, as he made his way to Richard's house.

"Wake up!" he cried, pounding at the door. "I'm ready."

"You've got to be joking," Richard called out sleepily.

By midafternoon Seth was up, confident, steady on his feet, balanced on his board. He and Richard were both on surfboards now. They had paddled out to the place where the swell would catch them, straddled the boards, facing the shore, while Richard taught him how to wait. Or tried to.

"That would have been a good one to go with," Seth said, as a wave crashed to the shore ahead of them.

"Not enough of a barrel," Richard said. "That's what you have to ride. Be careful not to get caught in the top of the wave, or it can slam you onto the sand. You can really get hurt that way. And keep your weight the way I showed you. One leg in front of the other, guiding, more weight on the one in front. Just going along with it. Like working a Ouija board."

"I can do that," Seth said. "I'm sort of psychic."

"Get ready." They both got to their knees. "Now!" Richard said.

And they were up, and gliding, and Seth was moving along with it, exhilarated. It was true, what Richard had said. Like riding the rays of the the moon. Rays that were invisible, whited out by the sunlight. But he could feel the pull, the gravity, as he lost gravity, became a part of the tide.

The sense of freedom, the grace, he'd felt before when he skied, the thrill of the effortless glide. But this was different. This was salt sprayed, no chilling wind against his cheeks, the sun on his body. He was free but connected, a part of the moon, a part of the universe.

He slid, standing, towards the shore. "All right!" he cried, exuberant. "All right!" he cried again, clambering to the beach, picking up the board, running toward Richard. "Let's go for it again."

"It would have been nice to have someone to eat lunch with," Karen said, when he finally got back to the room.

"Don't sulk," he said, as she sometimes said to him. "You want me to have a good time, don't you?"

"Not that good," she said. "You've been gone all day. You're burned."

"I'm brown," he said, flexing his pecs in front of the mirror, grinning at his reflection, the golden hair bleached nearly platinum now, curling around his face. There was a tiny dimple just below the side of his nose, in the smile line. "I've never been this dark. I look really handsome."

"Not that you're conceited," she said.

"My looks came from you and Dad. I'm not responsible. That would be braggadocio."

She put down the novel she had been reading. "What?"

"Braggadocio. Aren't you impressed?"

"Very."

"Richard taught me that. *And* how to be one with the tide. A truly amazing guy."

"Stop selling," she said. "Why are you selling so hard?"

"I want you to be happy," he said, the dimple disappearing.

"I appreciate that. Now go shower and get dressed for dinner. We're going to go see the Ramayana."

"Gee, I'm sorry. I made plans for dinner with Richard." He waited a moment. "But you're welcome to join us."

"You look really lovely," Richard said. "Pastels suit you."

"Don't try to sweet-talk her," said Seth, cutting into his *Baba Guling*. "She's in a very bad mood."

"I don't enjoy being coerced," Karen said. She could

feel the silk of her skirt against her naked legs, the warm, wet wind on her back. Bali was a feast for the senses, while it served you a feast for the belly, making you feel alive, even as you faltered in your convictions. You could taste the air, sweet, like a mango, the juiciness of it all but dripping from your lips.

"I can't believe I'm actually eating pig." Seth chewed. "The worst part is I like it. If I can enjoy eating pig, you can enjoy being coerced, Mom. Whatever that means."

"Blackmailed," said Karen.

The players of the gamelan moved into place, their costumes elaborate, bright red, laced with gold. The music started. Karen cocked her head and tried to follow the sweet discord.

Richard reached for her hand. She pulled away.

They were silent through most of the *Ramayana*, respectful of the performance. In Karen's case she was grateful not to have to make conversation. She could still feel Richard's touch on the back of her hand, gently searing, smell the light scent of Drakkar. Memory aroused her. Passion, once experienced, remembered, was, apparently, almost as provocative as the passion itself. Senses, robbing you of sense.

She could feel Richard staring at her profile, making her shift in her chair and sit up straighter, inviting his approval even as she scorned it. The raven-haired dancer in the pageant playing Sita, incarnation of beauty, wife of the hero king—her tiny body bound in shining fabric threaded with gold, wrapped fifteen times around her torso, making her seem even smaller, her hair twisted and knotted with gold—was spirited off by the lecherous usurper king, Ravena.

"Maybe you should do that to Mom," Seth murmured to Richard.

"Enough," Karen said, trying not to remember the taste of clove on his tongue.

"How can you be so insensible?" Seth asked her.

"Insensitive," Richard corrected. "Insensible, she'd have to be unconscious."

"Maybe you'd be better off," said Seth.

A dancer in a terrifying mask, with long false finger-nails, moved close to the audience. A little girl hid her face in her father's shirt.

"Well, I see that Old Metal-Mouth is staring at me with her usual longing." Seth wiped his mouth with his napkin, the careful way he'd observed Richard do it, and threw it on the table, backing up his chair. "I better give her a break." He got up.

"May I please be excused?" Karen coached him.

"Did you do something wrong?"

"Don't be a wise-ass," Richard said. "You're making her uncomfortable."

"You're both making me uncomfortable," she said. Yearning and frustration, a promise made she was desperately trying to keep, all condensed like clouds, bringing angry tears to her eyes. "I can't fight the two of you."

"I'll leave and give you better odds." Seth walked away.

"He's a really nice boy," Richard said. "You did a great job."

"You did a better one. How did you turn him around?"

"He turned himself. He obviously sees that we're good for each other." He touched the top of her hand, drummed softly on her fingers, the same rhythm chanted by the chattering men playing monkeys. She closed her eyes.

"Let's get out of here," he murmured.

"I made a promise to give you up."

"Well, you kept it. You gave me up." He leaned over, softly kissed her. "Now you're taking me back again."

Would it be all right? Now that Seth was safe, he himself urging her on, would it be pardonable to forgo the vow she'd made? Was she being disloyal to Charley?

How many times had she lain alone since Charley died? Was she condemned to be a little dead herself? Surely God would forgive her, if there were a God. If there were machinations in the universe, God had to be the Master Manipulator. Maybe this was all meant to be: destiny, design. Why would a god, if little gods ruled, fill her with juices, to have them dry up, untapped? Why would a great God have put her in a body, if her body were not to be enjoyed? And if her son, the one-day (maybe) teacher, with his tender intuition, reaching for the Invisible, was right, or even close, and everybody was God, had a spark of divinity in them, didn't she (She?) owe her Creation permission to be happy?

Richard kissed her once, just once, when they reached the sand. But once was all she needed to know what it moved in her.

Eight

TOURISTS in Bali were warned to watch their wallets. It was not the Balinese who were thieves but the monkeys. Packs of them, spoiled, brazen, ran through the forest named for them, came uninvited to cremations, stealing from offerings before they went on the funeral pyre. In the ancient temple of Uluwatu, far to the west, carved from the huge limestone rock it sat on, waves crashing against boulders far below, where visitors were advised they could see the most dramatic sunsets, monkeys ran up and down the steps filching Cokes from unwary hands, drinking thirstily, baptizing themselves with the dregs. Cameras were ripped from straps around necks, pockets were picked with a skill professionals would envy, coins kept but credit cards dumped down the cliff, as though the deft little robbers understood that their unauthorized use might be questioned.

The security guards patrolling the luxury hotels would not hurt them, sacred as they were, but made sure they kept their distance, prodding them off-property with long sticks of bamboo. Often the wily little creatures would seize the end aimed at them and get into a small tug-of-war, imagining, one could only suppose, that combat, like theft, was just another game for their amusement.

Frogs, however, like birds, being more diminutive than those Westerners were used to, sometimes barely bigger than the pebbles they moved among, were given the run, or more accurately, the hop of the place. Nestled among lotuses in ponds, hiding in the drains of swimming pools and plunge pools, they belched out blithe little sounds, unmolested.

But creatures, sacred or appealing, worshiped or merely tolerated, were beside the point at the Four Seasons Hotel at Jimbaran Bay. Luxury was a word, a state, created for humans. Superhumans, if strength were a matter of wealth, it seemed to Karen, as she got out of the taxi at the entrance. It was open, as many Bali buildings were open, without walls except for the one behind the desk. In the near distance was the sea, turquoise and aquamarine. But just in front of her was a huge slab of what seemed to be a mirror—marble it was, probably, but marble polished to so fine a shine that it reflected. And what it reflected was the ocean below, making one continuous expanse of glittering, liquid blue, so what few guests were visible in the entryway seemed to be walking on water.

If Bali were a mirror, as Richard had said in their early conversations, what was this a mirror of? Had these people come for vacation alone? Were they all just riding the surface? Unless you had a tour guide for the soul, a priest, a lover conducting you through the mysteries, might you not miss what it was Bali really had to offer? How much of what Richard said did he really believe or feel? Even as she thrilled to the beauty, the splendor around them, the heavy scent of flowers, and money, she wondered what he'd had to do to get a room.

Silently she censured herself for feeling the least bit skeptical. Wasn't this everything she'd wanted in a romance? And romance was what it was, dreamlike, sultry and soft as the subtle breeze that blew through the marble-floored, thatched-roof open courtyard, touching her cheek like the love she'd thought was vanished.

Now, visibly, he seemed ready to demonstrate the extent of his affection. Not simply passion, but caring. Going to so much trouble, giving her the idyll he'd imagined and somehow managed to bring into being. Somehow. How?

He looked absolutely boyish, triumphant, as he strode to the reception desk, a great carved length of coconut wood, behind it two beautiful Balinese girls, slender and unmistakably feminine even in uniform. Pride strengthened his posture, as he said his name. There seemed to be a firmer set to his features, a more convincing kind of self-satisfaction. He'd managed to deliver what he'd promised.

"I thought of going directly to the villa," he said to her

as he registered. "But I wanted to make sure you knew we were here legitimately, that I didn't just steal a key. Though that possibility *did* cross my mind."

"How did you do it?"

"Why, I sold my soul of course," he said, scratching with the pen, a flourish on his signature.

A buggy, a canvas-roofed golf cart, took them round the gently curving roads between trees and thatch-roofed villas to the villa that was to be theirs. The porter got out of the cart, sarong tight across his hips, shirt unwrinkled even in the heat, and taking his shoes off, unlocked the antique double doors. There was an open courtyard, set with stepping stones in between pebbles, with a great gray stone that seemed to be a shrine, yellow sarong wrapped discreetly around it, everything softened by green, a profusion of flowers.

To the right was an open area with a roof, a deep, batiked sofa, pillowed, with spare cushions, what the porter indicated as a minibar in a darkwood cupboard, a table set for two, atop it a bowl filled with mangosteens, passion fruit, tiny bananas and rambutan, the spiky specialty of Bali, which, opened, yielded a soft, pale green center like a grape. Richard pressed it between her lips.

"Careful," he said. "There's a pit in it."

"Like a lot of great adventures," Karen said, smiling, and let the sweet moistness burst in her mouth.

In front of them lay a small plunge pool, a giant stone fish spitting water into it, the far edge looking down at the sea. To the left was the villa itself, unlocked with the same key by the porter. Inside was a large double bed, mosquito netting strung around it from the ceiling, like a veil.

"Thank you," Richard said in Balinese to the porter, and then, in English: "We'll take it from here."

The porter clasped his hands together, and half bowing, left them. "And from here," Richard said, pointing to the bed. "And from there." He led her back out into the courtyard, and easing the backpack from his shoulders, reached for her fingers and pulled her onto the sofa.

"This is the first place I intend to take you," he said, loosing the buttons on her blouse. "In the Victorian sense."

"Ah," he sighed, a little later. "Sometimes they really knew what they were doing, those Victorians."

They did not dress for dinner. No matter how costly or elegant their accommodations, people rarely dressed up in Bali. Besides, she had brought no extra clothes, knowing she was there for only one night, and that, she imagined, to be spent in complete privacy. But they had swum in their plunge pool, and used it for what such small, warm, liquid places were doubtless intended for, making love so many times they were ravenous for more than just each other. He cut through the thick green skin of the mangosteen and fed her, one by one, the soft liquidy petals inside. But after a while they agreed they needed something substantial.

She brushed her hair and blew it dry with the hair-blower in the marble bathroom, and then blew his, combing it with her fingers. His hair was thicker than hers, not as silky, but it moved her more than it would have had it been soft. The slight coarseness touched her, making him somehow more vulnerable, because it was one of the few things about him that seemed inarguably strong. Not simply in the physical sense, because there was an enormous power in his body, the set of his shoulders, his chest, the contour of his thighs. But she understood how really exposed men were, how quickly Charley had vanished in spite of his imposing size, how defenseless Seth was for all his bravado.

Richard had brought a new T-shirt, and eased it from his backpack, along with her miniature keyboard. "What's this?" she said.

"I got it from Seth. I thought perhaps you might be inspired."

And she was. They had dinner on the candlelit terrace below, near the ocean's edge, where they could hear the gentle lapping. And in her head, it became song. As hungry as she'd been, as soon as she'd eaten her appetizer she was full.

She looked up from her plate. "Me, too," said Richard,

and signaling the waiter, canceled their main course and took her back to the villa.

The bed had been turned down for the evening, the mosquito netting loosed from its moorings so that it fell in whitely translucent folds around the mattress. Slippers had been laid out, one pair on either side of the bed, on a small stepstool.

And on the desk, in front of the miniature keyboard Richard had brought along, was placed a pyramid of orange marigolds, striped with purple zinnias, fruit and candied pink cakes and curled baby banana leaves circling its base. "How beautiful," she said. "They've given us flowers."

"They're not for us," said Richard. "It's an offering for your keyboard. So the gods of the keyboard will be good to you. Play something for me."

"It's been so long," she said.

"Try." He put his arm around her bare, warm shoulders.

"Hoagy Carmichael said that the notes are all already there, the song is already in the keys, and whoever finds it first gets to keep it."

"I don't know who Hoagy Carmichael is."

"He wrote 'Stardust.' If you don't know what that is, don't tell me." She turned on the machine. Struck a programmed, automatic chord. And her heart filled, and the fullness moved to her throat. And a song came out of her.

She sang bits of it to him as they danced around the plunge pool, and then jumped in, bodies entwining, merging in the water. She sang it till he knew a little of it, too, and sang it with her. He had a not very good voice, but there was sweetness in his trying. Then he lifted her from the pool and carried her inside the bedroom, still dripping, toweled her off on the bed. He kissed her once, lightly, before going to the wall and turning the switch that spun the blades of the wooden ceiling fan. Then, with a second click, he turned to her, triumphant, and said, as though it were his own song: "Air-con."

They lay in the cool and watched the slow-moving fan on the ceiling. "It would be lovely to be here with you like this forever," he said.

"Come home with me." She hadn't meant to say it, but she'd known all along she would.

"I said 'here.' "

"You said 'forever.' "

"It's unrealistic. You know the kind of man I am."

"The kind of man you *were*. People change."

"Don't bet on it."

"Do you love me?"

"You great, soft lump," he said, and kissed her. "How could I not?"

"Then come home with me," she said.

"Idylls are idylls because they end. And they're not all that easy to arrange."

She looked around at the indisputable grandeur. "How did you manage?"

He didn't answer.

When the sun was first rising in the early morning, he took her to their private lanai, with its outdoor shower, a bamboo spout pouring water onto their heads. He scrubbed her and oiled her, lathered her hair, rubbed strong fingers against her skull, tattooed the back of her neck with his thumbs. From where they stood beneath the shower, they could see the planes taking off from the airfield.

She had already called the airline, tiptoeing to the out-side phone as he dozed, to make sure there was room for him on the plane.

"Wait here," he said in the marble-floored entry, as he went to settle the bill.

"Why? Are you paying with some old girlfriend's jewelry?" she said, jokingly.

He blanched, the curious lack of color that manifested whenever talk touched on failure, disgrace, the loss of the lives on the river. It was a quick change of pigment that drained his face, as young women might blush.

"I was only joking," she said, as her son often said he was only joking when he hit something too close to the mark he hadn't really known was there.

"I am paying in cash," Richard said. He made the announcement with the vanished hauteur that had laced his voice on occasion at the start of their relationship. From the very first meeting, in spite of how attractive she'd thought him, she sensed something cavalier: a layer of overweening pride. Beneath the charming surface lay a stubborn inability to deal with being less than he wanted to be, in spite of his pretense that his Bali life was all that he wished for. That a grown man could buzz through impenetrable traffic on a secondhand Vespa, when his whole nature cried out for a car. She saw him for a moment absolutely clearly, unable to face his own weakness, just as she was embarrassed to deal with her strength. For all that the world was supposed to have changed, strength was still considered unbecoming in women.

But didn't she have spine enough for both of them? Hadn't she shown, even to herself, the stuff she was made of when Charley died? Hadn't she proved she could go on alone, whether or not she wanted to?

Wasn't the only lack in her life a lover? Now that she had found Richard, why did he have to be more than he was? Didn't she love him, in spite of his caution that she wasn't to love him? Hadn't the wastefulness of his youth been acknowledged, repented; hadn't he made amends with his exile, the pain of losing his family's love? Hadn't he done enough penance for the accident, wearing the sackcloth of his shame? And wasn't it a woman's job, really, to forgive, to nurture, to heal? What could he have possibly done that was unforgivable?

Richard paid the bill in Australian dollars. She did not question, except in the back of her mind, why he should have that particular currency. What he had bought her in the way of reasonably priced meals at his beach restaurant had been paid for in local *rupiah*, inflated to such a level that it had distended his fanny-pack. As she stood beside him now at the cashier's desk of the hotel, and loved him, convinced she really loved him, delighting in his nearness, still heady from his touch, his clean, manly smell, remembering how connected they had been, how connected she still felt to him, stirred by the certainty he would be leaving the island with her, her mind stepped a little aside.

And wondered where the money came from.

"Did you have a great time?" Seth asked her when she got back to their villa. "Was it the best time you ever had?" There was great animation in his questioning, obvious, openhearted affection, no trace of the possessiveness that had rankled in the beginning.

"What did you do while I was gone?" she asked, not ready to make him a partner in her feelings, uncomfortable with that much sharing with her son. He was, after all, her child, not a partner. To have him know details of her amorous adventures would be disturbing, especially as she felt the slightest bit disloyal: So powerfully erotic had the time with Richard been that she hadn't even thought about Charley.

"I hung out with the Bramsons. It was their last night, so I thought I'd give Jennifer a break. I tried to pick up the tab for dinner, but her dad wouldn't let me. You wouldn't have minded my doing that, would you?"

"Not at all," she said. "Very gentlemanly. Gallant." She gave it a European inflection, emphasis on the second syllable, so it sounded even more noble than it was.

"Yeah, well, that's me all over. Gallant," he said, mimicking her emphasis. He was standing in front of the bathroom mirror, naked to the waist, flexing, his forearm held with the opposite hand while he pressed. "Gallant and incredibly muscular, not to mention the tan. How about this tan? She could hardly keep her braces off me."

He changed arms and flexed again, this time on the other side. "I'm going to be the sensation of the Upper West Side." He lifted his arms above his head, checked the white beneath his armpits. "I better tan these up. I can't believe we're going home. It feels like we only just got here. Bali time, like Richard said. Slowed down, and forever, but all the same it passes."

"You want to invite the Bramsons to lunch?"

"They're gone," he said. "They left this morning. But they invited me to come to Sydney."

"That's lovely. Maybe you can visit them one vacation."

"I have no real wish to go to Australia. Their best equipment comes from Japan. They have a hard time understanding real state of the art because they're so caught in state of the Asia. So are you the happiest you've ever been?"

"I'm very happy, thank you."

"You look happy. You look really good. Really young."

"The highest compliment," Karen said.

"Not as if you were ever looking old," he said. "It's just that this place has done wonders for you. I wish we didn't have to leave."

"You have school."

"Bali is a better school," he said, and half crouching,

maneuvered the waves that weren't beneath him, making ocean sounds, gently roaring, the motors of nature humming in his throat. "I'm really learning how to wait."

"That's good," Karen said.

"But it's not good to wait too long. I got caught in a wave yesterday, the top of it, the way Richard told me not to. Over the falls, they call it, these surfers. That's what it feels like. Niagara without the barrel. I mean, I did a somersault, so my legs went over my neck and slammed me down so hard on the sand, I thought I was going to be paralyzed."

"Don't surf anymore," she said, as calmly as she could, panicked at the thought that something might have happened to him.

"Oh, Mom, don't be such a wuss. I'm a survivor. And Richard can keep on coaching me."

"We have to go home."

He hesitated, half closing his eyes, as if he were reflecting deeply. And then: "I think he should come home with us."

"Really?" she said, elation mixing with relief. She had been wondering how to put the idea to him.

"Totally. I was sort of standing in the way for a while, but I see how good he is for you. You're blooming. You had a good time where he took you, didn't you?"

"I did," she said.

"The best time ever?"

"A better time than I've had in a long time." Ever, she

couldn't quite say. Eager as Seth seemed to hear those words, there might be a boomerang later, a return to re-sentment if he considered she had completely set aside his father.

"Well, the good times should continue," he mused, professorial, his hands folded over his chest. "Let the good times roll. Can I invite him to come home with us? He doesn't really have all that much here. I mean he can talk about the luxury of the sky and all, but I bet he'd really enjoy New York, and being . . ."—he swallowed—". . . part of a family. Can I ask him?"

"If you want," she said.

"I do." He went to the phone and lifted the receiver. "If you don't want him living in your room, he can stay in mine."

It was not until they were almost all packed, nothing left out but bathing suits, their toiletries, what they would wear for dinner and need on the plane, that she noticed the stereo equipment was missing. "Where's your CD player?" she asked Seth.

"Oh, that," he said, in a tone that struck her as just a touch too casual.

"Yes, that."

"I must have left it on the beach or something."

"On the beach?" she said, disbelievingly.

"I'll go out and look for it." He started toward the door.

"I know what that equipment means to you," she said. "You wouldn't have left it on the beach."

He shrugged. "Oh. Okay. I gave it to Jennifer."

"You did what?"

"Well, they don't have anything close to that in Australia. I told you. They have no real concept of state of the art."

"You *gave* it to Jennifer?"

"She really went kind of nuts over it."

"You *gave* it to Jennifer?"

"Okay. I sold it to Jennifer."

"And where's the money?"

"I spent it."

"How?"

He looked away.

"You gave it to Richard," she said. "For the hotel."

"We wanted you to have a good time," he said, miserably.

She ran down the beach with a fury that left her oblivious to the heat of the sand underfoot, to the searing sun, the difficult time of day. It was an hour when even native Balinese crouched in huts, gave massages on tables that were little more than pieces of plastic strung over wood, manicures under dried palm leaves fashioned into thatch, temporary roofs.

She burst through the gates that led to Richard's garden. Garden, she thought contemptuously. So irresponsible, so negligent and unreliable, he could not even tend to and prune what nature had given him as a gift.

"You can stop your packing," she said through his open door, his pathetic little oven of a hut. It was all he deserved, she could not help thinking now. What he had earned.

"Why?" he said happily, folding his clothes, a soft bag big enough to hold his meager pile of belongings waiting beside them on the bed. "Are we going to go shopping in New York?"

"You got the money from my son," she said icily. "You paid for the hotel with money from my son."

He went pale again, suddenly, the truth transparent, blood that had been noble only in the pages of Burke's *Peerage* drained from his face. "I never asked him for it. He volunteered."

"You took money from my son. From a *kid*. You made what we had into something sordid."

"Oh, come now." He tried for a smile. "Everything matters so much to you. *Nothing* matters that much. It's about *life*, Karen. Living it. He wanted you to have a good time. I should have managed it on my own, eventually, but there weren't enough days."

"You said you sold your soul. But you didn't. You sold my son's. You sold mine."

"You said you loved me." He was pleading now with his eyes, even while his words were unyielding. "I warned you not to care too much. But you *would* fall in love."

"That's *my* character flaw."

"Well, mine is I haven't any." His skin looked ashen, signaling his weakness, even as his words became strong. "I told you from the outset the kind of man I was. You were the one who needed a hero."

"Not a hero. Just a man."

"Oh, come off it. You want everything to be more than it is. You weren't content to let this be an interlude. *You* had to make it a love story." Angrily, he started taking the clothes out of his bag.

"It *was* a love story."

"You don't know what love is. You think you do, because you invest so much of yourself in what you're feeling. But when you love somebody, you love them how they are, with all their flaws, with all their weaknesses."

"Not when they use your son."

"Your son knows what love is better than you," he said sadly. "He wanted you to be happy."

Nine

"MO-OM . . ." Seth said, as she lay on her bed, a wet cloth over her eyes.

She'd run back to their hotel and collapsed on the bed. "Go away."

"You're taking this all *much* too seriously."

"You lied to me," she said. "For the first time in your life you lied."

"Well, it wasn't exactly the first time," he said, sitting on the bed beside her. "I changed a grade once on my report card. Dad almost kicked the shit out of me."

She took the cloth from her eyes. "When was that?"

"Fourth grade," he said. "My handwriting wasn't very good, so it was hard to be a forger."

"He never told me," Karen said.

"Yeah, well, Dad was my bud. We were partners in crime."

"Not such a big crime. You never did it again, did you?"

"No . . ." He measured his words. "This wasn't such a crime either."

"Richard took money from you. To pay for . . ." She couldn't finish the phrase. What had felt exalted now seemed licentious. "It's worse than taking candy from a baby."

"What's the big deal about candy? From what they know now about sugar, a baby is better off without it."

"He made you lie."

"No, he didn't. He didn't ask me for the money, or tell me not to tell you. It was my idea. If I loved somebody, and I couldn't afford a honeymoon, you'd help me out, wouldn't you?"

She sat up. "It's my hope you will earn your own way."

"Well, I will," he said. "But if that happened, if I fell in love before my life was really luxe, and I wasn't a successful entrepreneur yet, or a media mogul, which I'm considering being, you'd lend me a hand. Wouldn't you?"

"I suppose."

"I *know*. You'd do it, because you love me."

"Yes, I do."

"Then what's the problem?"

"There is no problem. It's over."

"He's not coming with us?" Seth looked stricken.

"I'm sure he wouldn't, even if I wanted him to."

"That's because he's too proud. It's braggadocio. But you want him to, don't you?"

"I don't think it's a good idea."

"Why not?"

"He has no spine. No sense of purpose."

"Maybe he never had a reason to. But now he does. He can learn self-respect, because somebody excellent really cares for him."

"Well, thank you for that, at least," she said.

"I meant *me,*" he said, and laughed, and kissed her, and went to get Richard.

The afternoon was overcast. Richard came with a surfboard, laid it in the courtyard, set Seth to waxing it. The boy pretended concentration on his assigned task, trying not to seem as though he wanted to listen to what was going on inside the room, leaning only a little toward the closed glass doors.

"You were right," Karen said to Richard. "When you love somebody, you love them as they are."

"Don't back down." Richard sat on the couch. "It would never have worked. What happened with us was only for Bali. If we left Bali, the magic would be gone, too. So we'll leave it as it is. That way it will stay perfect."

"You're punishing me, because I said angry things."

"They were true," said Richard. "I told you I haven't

any character. Even letting myself agree to go with you was
because you're stronger than I am. Smarter. You'd get tired
of that after a while."

"I made a mistake," she pleaded. "Forgive me."

"There's nothing to forgive. I had a beautiful time. I
hope you did, too. But there's an end to it. We'd get back
to your world, and it would only be a matter of time. You'd
have all your clever, accomplished friends, and they'd say
'What does *he* do?' Americans are like that, you know."

"You could get a job."

"Doing what? Teaching surfing? A teller in a bank,
with recommendations from Lord Hensley?"

"You could find something. With your charm . . ."

"My charm," he said. "How long do you think it
would be before you started to despise me? Before I despised myself, and started chasing after other women, just to
hurt you, just to reassure myself I hadn't lost my 'charm.' "

"You're more than you think you are."

"I know *exactly* what I am. It was a holiday. Holidays
end. Let's just leave it. That way, we'll always love each
other."

"You do love me?"

"Of course I do, you great soft lump. I'm only a scoundrel, not a fool."

"Oh, Richard." She knelt by the couch where he sat
and put her head in his lap. "Don't throw us away."

"But, my darling, I'm not," he said, and lifted her face,

bent so that his words, the clove-scented breath behind them, brushed her lips. "I'm saving us."

"Come," he said, taking her by the hand, reaching out to Seth as they went onto the terrace. "They're having a ceremony on the beach. We should watch it together. The proper good-bye to Bali."

Numbly, mutely, she fell into step behind them, her beautiful boys. Seth walked next to Richard, tanned dark as he was now. Their hair, lightened by the sun, was nearly the same shade, Seth's thick curls shadowing his cheeks with ringlets, still about him an aura of baby angel, one of the *putti* that clung to the ceilings of Italian chapels. They could have been brothers, Karen thought, the young one and the older one.

Something strained at her heart, her whole body, pulled at her womb. Farther down the beach lovers walked, arm in arm; it hurt as it had hurt to see couples arm in arm after Charley's death, loss, anticipated in this case, as painful as loss that had already occurred.

A yellow canopy with jeweled fringes set on stakes in the sand flapped in the intensifying breeze. A priest in saffron robes held a naked baby under it, slipped golden bangles onto its tiny wrists, clipped golden earrings on its ears. Behind them on the sand sat the relatives, dressed in their worshipful finery, lace blouses and sarongs, the men similarly adorned. Food-and flower-laden offerings were floated into the sea.

"Someone's carried that baby from the day it was born," Richard said. "They don't ever set it down, or let it touch the ground, because it's still so open, evil spirits might invade it. This ritual comes when it's old enough to deal with the dark forces in the earth."

The priest bathed the child in holy water. Carefully taking the tiny foot, he pressed it into the sand.

"You should have done that with me," Seth said to his mother. "You should have carried me from the day I was born, and then I wouldn't have spent so much of my life invaded by evil spirits." He was grinning so she'd know he was joking.

"One last swim," Seth said, giving Richard his towel, and ran into the water.

They watched him splashing out through the shallows. "Why are you being so stubborn?" Karen asked Richard.

"A stiff backbone is better than none."

"You make me ashamed." She was more than ashamed. She felt bereft. She had spoiled it herself with anger, too quick words.

"Don't be. You're really quite a woman. You've taught me to stand my ground. That's more than I've known how to do my whole life."

"But I love you," she said.

"And I you." He put his hand on her shoulder, turned her, lifted her face to kiss. "Now it will stay like this for-ever."

She went back to the room to finish packing, leaving Richard to supervise Seth. She'd been gone a few minutes when the wind came up. Whistles blew. Warning flags were set into the sand. Swimmers and surfers who heard the shrillness over the howl of the wind started heading for the beach.

Richard signaled Seth to come in to shore, calling to him as loudly as he could. But the wind was overpowering in its sound. And though Richard had caught Seth's eye, the boy seemed to see Richard's wave as salute, a greeting. He started waving in return, his golden head bobbing above the waves, as a friend would signal "Hi."

And then he wasn't there anymore.

The story about the Balinese facing up to the Dutch, as an example of human nature ennobling itself for the sake of an ideal, honor, a sacrifice meant to preserve, was one that Richard had never quite gotten the point of, even as he told it. Having been throughout his life without any guid-ing principle, selflessness was outside his comprehension. Still, as it was a riveting tale, and a true one, he told it as part of his tours, as he had to Karen and Seth, even while admitting that he considered the sacrifice silly.

He swam through the water now to the place where he'd seen the boy disappear, and dove through the churning waters. He saw Seth flailing, bubbles coming from his mouth and nose, fighting against the undertow, being dragged toward the coral reef. All at once Richard understood what it was to care, to prize, to want to preserve.

He reached Seth, grabbed him, struggled with him, towed him away from the reef, up to the surface, pulled him toward the beach. A pair of surfers still rode the turbulent waters, and Richard called out to them. He swam the boy over, handed him up. They took Seth by the arms, held him between their boards, and paddled him toward the shore.

"Lost," cried the Balinese man, as he ran along the sand beside Karen.

She raced down the beach, hardly able to breathe. In the distance she could see people gathering, the grim semicircle that signaled accident, disaster.

"Lost," moaned the Balinese man, running ahead of her now.

Dread seized her. Even as she ran, she felt the prescience of doom. Grief grabbed her heart with fortified fingers: the feeling a known one to her now.

Was her boy lost? Was life so capricious that it gave you things you longed for, only to take them, like the torrent of the ocean, pulling all you prized away? What was there you could hold onto, or was it all just a string of losses? Youth, beauty, love. How could you even keep what you thought you were?

She reached the place where the crowd was, broke through. She saw Seth lying on his stomach, choking, spewing up water. One of the surfers straddled him, rhythmically pressing his ribs. A second surfer stood gazing out to sea.

"Lost," keened the Balinese man, and wept for all his own losses.

Karen ran to her son and knelt beside him, touched the matted hair, pressed her face close to his. "Oh, my darling," she said, and started to cry. "Thank God."

"He saved me," Seth murmured.

Her eyes searched the crowd for Richard. She called out his name. "Richard?"

There was a moment of terrible silence, and the ratcheting of the wind. Then the surfer saw something in the water, and rushed into the shallows, amid the roiling of rocks and pebbles and sand. He pulled the big man up onto the beach.

"Richard!" she screamed, and ran to him.

The surfer turned him over. His body was scraped and scratched from the beating of the stones. He choked, water coming from his mouth and nose.

"You're alive," she wept, and fell to the sand beside him.

"Seth?" he asked.

"You saved him."

"Holy Christ," he said, and managed a smile. "You *did* it. You made me a hero."

"So it's settled then," she said, as she wiped the last of his scrapes and wounds, and draped soft towels around the bruises on his shoulders. "You're coming with us."

"No, I'm not," Richard said. "Nothing's changed."

"Everything's changed. *You've* changed."

"I'm still a bad penny. That hasn't changed. But for once in my life I thought of someone besides myself," he said. "Grant me the grace to do that twice."

"Well, if you ask me you're both pretty stupid," Seth said at the airport. "I never want to be an adult."

"Neither do I," said Richard, and hugged him.

"When you save somebody's life you have an obligation to take care of them. I read that in one of the books on Bali."

"I *am* taking care of you. *And* your mother." He took the Bali coin on the leather thread around his neck and slipped it over Seth's head. "Making sure you both have the life you ought to have."

"Who are you to decide?" Seth said angrily, pulling away, moving toward the gate.

Richard turned to Karen. "He'll forgive me after a while. You can teach him the wisdom of what I've done."

"How?" she said, and the tears started. "How, when I don't understand it myself?"

"You will when you meet the man who deserves you," Richard said, and kissed her tears.

"Maybe we could go next year to Bali," Seth said, looking out the window at the lush green island far below.

"Maybe."

"Or maybe you could send him a ticket, and he'll change his mind."

"I don't think so."

"Maybe he never really loved either of us," Seth said sadly.

"Of course he did."

"Then how could he let us go?"

"Because that's how life is. You meet somebody, and you love them, and then you say good-bye."

"I hate that."

"So do I," said Karen. "But that's what you have to learn to do."

Sometimes, when she passes a travel agency, she looks in the window and searches for a poster of Bali. Sometimes, when she waits late at night alone, she picks up the telephone and starts to call him, but hangs up. Sometimes she sits at the piano and works on perfecting the song she began on the keyboard, with the flowery offering in front of it coaxing the gods into giving her music. That there is music back in her life is a gift she is not convinced came from the gods.

Sometimes, when she dreams, she dreams of Richard walking on the sand, beneath the stars, remembering their boundless intimacy, as they were in Bali. Not just how many there were, but how surprising, unearthly, as Westerners were used to them: the Southern Cross, a whole different set of stars, new stars, shooting stars, more than a canopy of stars, closer to an embrace. In her dream, Richard is deep in conversation with Charley, who agrees that what she is is a great soft lump, sentimental to her core.

And Charley chastises Richard because Richard could be there when she wakes up, but Charley can't. And Richard confesses that he can't be there either, not like Charley was there for her, that sooner than later he'd be off with another woman, and that would never do. And she says in her sleep, "You're right," and wakes herself.

It is a recurring dream, so she thinks of talking it over

with a therapist, except that it's very clear: She understands what it means. She has no secrets from herself.

But she has joined a gym so she'll still be fit if the right man comes along. And she has noted a very pleasant-seeming fellow on the treadmill every afternoon at six when he would be going home if he had one. He watches her from the corner of his eye, and, casual as he tries to make the observation seem, it is clear he has great interest. He wears no wedding ring.

GWEN DAVIS is a novelist, and a traveler. One of the places she loves is Bali, the setting for *LOVESONG*. Widowed, she raised her two children in California. She has lately resided in Paris, writing travel pieces for *The Wall Street Journal* and has her eye on Ireland as her next stop.